...nge day had taught Olivia anything,
...hat she had been lying to herself about
...feelings. She had never really fallen out of
...ove with Jackson. The realisation hit her like a
thunderbolt. *Maybe I never will.*

But she still lived in Franklin Grove. He still
travelled from movie set to movie set. None of
the issues that had split them apart had changed.

They might still seem perfect for each other . . .
but could it ever *really* work?

Sink your fangs into these:

MY SISTER THE VAMPIRE

MY BROTHER THE WEREWOLF

Sienna Mercer

MY SISTER THE VAMPIRE

DOUBLE DISASTER!

EGMONT

With special thanks to Stephanie Burgis

For Rhiannon, with love. May you have lots of adventures!

EGMONT

We bring stories to life

My Sister the Vampire: Double Disaster! first published in Great Britain 2013
by Egmont UK Limited
The Yellow Building, 1 Nicholas Road, London W11 4AN

Copyright © Working Partners Ltd 2013
Created by Working Partners Limited, London WC1X 9HH

ISBN 978 1 4052 6570 6

1 3 5 7 9 10 8 6 4 2

A CIP catalogue record for this title is available from the British Library

Typeset by Avon DataSet Ltd, Bidford on Avon, Warwickshire
Printed and bound in Great Britain by the CPI Group

54091/1

EGMONT LUCKY COIN

Our story began over a century ago, when seventeen-year-old
Egmont Harald Petersen found a coin in the street.

He was on his way to buy a flyswatter, a small hand-operated
printing machine that he then set up in his tiny apartment.

The coin brought him such good luck that today Egmont has
offices in over 30 countries around the world. And that lucky
coin is still kept at the company's head offices in Denmark.

Chapter One

O h my darkness!' Ivy Vega collapsed on to her front doorstep with a moan. Resting her elbows on the knees of her black combat trousers, she sighed. 'I have never been so happy to be finished with a party.'

'Wasn't it wonderful, though?' said her twin sister, Olivia Abbott, who sat down beside her. They were identical, apart from the fact that Olivia was grinning happily, and favoured clothes like the bright pink skirt she was now rearranging.

Oh, and also the fact that Olivia was human, while Ivy was a vampire.

'I couldn't believe how perfectly it all went!' Olivia said.

'Are you kidding?' Ivy snorted. 'Groomzilla was in charge, remember? *Nothing* was going to go wrong.'

Yesterday, their dad had married Lillian Margolis, the glamorous vampire movie director. The twins had met her just a year earlier, when a huge Hollywood movie had come to film in tiny Franklin Grove. Ivy couldn't have been happier for her dad – Lillian was the perfect addition to their family – but the memory of his frantic wedding preparation was enough to make her shudder.

How many weeks had it taken her dad to settle on exactly the right trim for the place cards at the reception tables? Ivy winced at the memory. *I think I'd rather eat garlic than ever have to see another wedding invitation ever again!*

It was no wonder she was exhausted now! Ivy

shook her head at her sister. 'How can you still be so perky? You may live in a different house, but I know you didn't escape *that* much prep work.'

'And it all paid off, every bit of it.' Olivia swayed side to side, smiling dreamily. 'Wasn't it just the most romantic day ever? All those gorgeous colours – do you remember that peach and silver swag?'

'*Remember* it?' Ivy let out a groan. 'I have *nightmares* about it! They accidentally delivered the wrong colour the first time round. Dad almost *fainted* from shock when he saw them. He ended up leaning against the wall, saying that he actually *hoped* he had gone colour-blind. If I hadn't threatened to tip Strawberry HemoGlobules on to my bridesmaid's dress, I'm not sure he would have snapped out of it!'

'He really came good in the end, though, didn't he?' Olivia stretched out her legs, her pink toenail polish sparkling in the sunlight. 'I can't think of a better wedding planner. Even the peonies on the tables matched the colour scheme!'

Ivy felt her left eyelid begin to twitch dangerously. She wasn't sure she could take any more wedding talk – especially now that the actual wedding was over. *Calm down*, she told herself. *This nightmare can't go on forever!*

'Yes indeed,' she said dryly. 'I may never stop swooning over the memories of the . . . "awesome" colour scheme.'

'Oh, come on.' Laughing, Olivia dug her in the ribs. 'It was a day to remember! Even *you* have to admit that's true.'

'Well . . .' Ivy sighed. 'OK . . . It did kind of suck. In the good way. *Kinda*.'

'See?' Olivia beamed. 'You had *fu-u-u-u-un* . . .' Her last word broke off into a wide yawn.

'Aha!' Ivy shot upright and pointed triumphantly. 'I *knew* it. You're exhausted too!'

Olivia yawned again, not even *trying* to stifle

it this time. 'OK, you're right. I never imagined that being a bridesmaid would be such hard *work*.'

'You're telling me.' Ivy shook her head as she picked up all the confetti that had fallen from her hair on to her combat trousers. 'Is this stuff made out of glue, or something? I've showered twice this morning, and I still haven't got it all out!'

'Aww.' Olivia grabbed her arm, forcing her to look up. 'Did you ever think you'd see that?'

Ivy blinked, then blinked again as she looked where her twin was pointing. On the pavement in front of them, their dad, their new stepmom and their grandparents were all negotiating the 'awkward goodbye'. Their grandparents would soon be heading back to Transylvania, home of the elite, upper-class vampire society.

'Wow,' Ivy breathed. 'Is that really Dad?'

Charles Vega normally looked really

uncomfortable around any type of 'goodbye' – but not today! He was beaming as Lillian smiled serenely at his side.

Olivia shook her head. 'Lillian has really had an effect on him. I guess love can work miracles.'

Under Ivy's disbelieving gaze, Charles stepped forward and, as if it were the most natural thing in the world, pulled his parents into a hug.

Ivy's mouth dropped open. She was still staring, dumbstruck, when her dad turned around.

'Come on, girls,' he said. 'Say goodbye to your grandparents!'

Ivy jumped up. *That, I can do!* She and Olivia rushed together down the stairs to give their grandparents big hugs of their own.

As Olivia hugged their grandfather, Ivy buried her face into her grandmother's shoulder. The Countess stroked her hair, and Ivy could have somersaulted for joy.

I'm so glad she's finally forgiven me.

Her grandparents had pleaded with Ivy to attend Wallachia Academy, an elite vampire finishing school in Transylvania. Ivy had gone along and tried her very best to fit in with the other students, but in the end she'd had to abandon the snooty academy – she'd missed her home too much. Her grandparents had both been appalled – and for a while, Ivy had really feared she'd lost her grandmother's love for good.

'I am really, truly proud of you,' the Countess whispered into Ivy's ear.

Ivy was glad she had her face hidden, because she was feeling very *un-vampire-y* tears welling up in her eyes. *OK, no sappiness.* She took a deep breath and stepped back, making a show of looking around. 'Hey, where's Horatio?'

'I don't know.' The Countess frowned. 'Where *is* Horatio?'

Olivia giggled. 'Um . . .'

Smiling, Charles shook his head and pointed. 'We should have known.'

The Count and Countess's vampire butler was two doors down on Undertaker Hill, stalking Ivy's neighbour Mr Galloway around his car, which was covered with soap suds.

'What in the name of darkness is he doing?' demanded the Count, his grey moustache bristling.

Ivy's lips twitched into a grin. 'Do you really have to ask?'

Mr Galloway's voice drifted down the street. 'But I told you, I really don't need any help washing my car!'

'Let me, sir.' Horatio pinched the sponge from their neighbour's hands with his vampire strength. 'I must insist.'

Ivy cringed as she saw the outraged expression on Mr Galloway's face. He stepped forward threateningly. 'Look, you . . . Hey!' His mouth dropped open as he leaned in to watch Horatio sweep the sponge around with professional precision. 'How are you doing *that*?'

'It is a special, spiralling, counter-clockwise technique – I invented it myself!' Horatio coughed modestly and stepped back to demonstrate. 'You see? Much more effective!'

'Well, I'll be . . .' Mr Galloway's scowl transformed into a smile as he saw the gleaming paintwork. 'That actually *is* impressive!'

'Thank you, sir. And now, if you'll allow me . . .' Smiling with quiet pride, Horatio straightened and removed his jacket. 'There is some serious work to be done here. Although . . .' He paused. 'Yes, this would be much easier if we use some of my special, homemade turtle wax.'

Mr Galloway choked. 'Your *what*?'

'I have some just here, in the car.' Frowning with concentration, Horatio hurried over to the hire car that he would be driving back to the airport. He opened the boot . . . then paused, suddenly looking anguished.

Uh-oh, Ivy thought. She didn't often see the dignified butler lose his cool! She sidled up to him as discreetly as she could, glancing down into the boot. Unsurprisingly, the luggage was arranged like a 3D puzzle, every suitcase perfectly placed. *He certainly can't be upset about his packing!*

'Is everything OK?' she whispered.

Horatio shook his head, still gazing with obvious desperation at the jigsaw-like stack of luggage. 'If I'm going to use my special turtle wax, I'll have to take it out of my suitcase,' he whispered, his voice cracking. 'But my suitcase is beneath the Count and Countess's luggage – at the bottom of the boot.'

'Uh . . . so?' Ivy shrugged. 'Can't you just dig it out and then re-pack?'

Horatio turned on her with a look so appalled, it actually rivalled Olivia's expression the time

10

Ivy had suggested Olivia wear a paisley skirt with her plaid blouse.

Ivy blinked and stepped back. 'Or . . . not?'

Horatio pointed at the boot with a finger that trembled. 'Look at that, Miss Ivy.'

'Er . . .' Ivy shrugged again. 'All I see is packed suitcases.'

'No . . .' Horatio shook his head with obvious disappointment. 'What you see are *perfectly* packed suitcases!' A look of rapt passion spread across his face as he continued. 'This is the Platonic *ideal* of suitcase-packing! They can be easily removed from the boot once we reach the airport, yet they are secure enough that no damage will be incurred to *any* items while driving. I have *dreamed* my whole life of managing to pack with such precision, such perfection.'

'Oh.' Ivy gulped, looking again at the suitcases. 'Um. Oh, the, er . . . tectonic ideal. Right. Sorry I didn't realise. Should I take a picture?'

'There is no need.' Horatio shook his head. 'I will never forget the day I displayed such excellence in my craft. I couldn't. And I planned to tell my fiancée, Helga, all about it once I had returned to Transylvania.' His expression crumpled. 'But I cannot if I must destroy it before we even leave for the airport!'

'And speaking of which . . .' The Countess was suddenly standing beside them, giving him a stern look that made Ivy take another step back. When her grandmother looked like this – confident, powerful and seriously scary – it was suddenly easy to remember that she was one of the oldest and most powerful vampires in the world.

'We are taking a *commercial* flight, Horatio,' the Countess said, sounding as if the word 'commercial' was actually painful on her tongue. 'That means that we are on someone *else*'s timetable.'

Oops. From the tone of her grandmother's

voice, Ivy could tell that wasn't something the Countess was used to . . . and she obviously did *not* like it.

'Of course, Madam.' Horatio's shoulders slumped as he turned back to Mr Galloway. 'I do beg your pardon, sir,' he called, 'but I shan't be able to use my special turtle wax after all.' His voice trembled with emotion. 'You cannot *possibly* know how much I regret this. I will post some to you the very moment I return home, however. Such a fine vehicle deserves only the best. If only –'

'Oh, Horatio!' Ivy couldn't wait any longer. She threw her arms around the tall butler, overcome by affection. 'I'm going to miss you so much.'

His arms closed around her, warm and reassuring. 'And I you, Miss Ivy,' he said. 'Do take good care of yourself.'

'I will,' she promised. Over his shoulder, she could see Olivia giving a fierce hug to their grandmother, who looked surprised and pleased. Mr Vega looked on, nodding approvingly. It was hard to imagine that, just a year ago, their family had been so awkward around each other.

But now, they were beginning to feel like a *real* family.

A moment later, the Transylvanians were all sitting, dignified and straight-backed, in Horatio's car, heading off towards the airport. As Ivy finished waving them away, she absently ran her hand through her hair . . . then groaned, as yet more confetti showered down around her shoulders.

Seriously? Where is this stuff even coming from?

That night at the Meat and Greet, the atmosphere was subdued. It had been well over ten minutes since the group arrived, without any waitress appearing to take their orders, but no one at the table had uttered a word of complaint. In fact, they'd barely spoken. As Olivia looked around at the three long faces, she shook her head. 'I can't believe my three *vampire* friends are all watching the sunset with dread in their eyes.'

Ivy's boyfriend, Brendan, just sighed, his dark hair flopping over his forehead. Her best friend, Sophia, looked miserable even in her usual fashionista glamour, with black rhinestone earrings falling nearly to her shoulders, as she intoned gloomily:

'It's the *last* sunset.'

Olivia frowned at Ivy, who gave back half a death-squint. 'Don't you get it?' Ivy asked. 'Tomorrow, *everything changes.*' She gestured sweepingly, making the bat ring on her left hand glint. 'Tomorrow, the grass becomes blue and the sky becomes green. Tomorrow, things that always made sense just . . . *stop*!'

'She's right,' Brendan mumbled. 'Because tomorrow . . .'

'We start ninth grade,' Sophia finished. She looked as if she might be sick. '*High school.*'

'Oh, come on!' Olivia tried to smile at everyone. 'Isn't it . . . "un-vampire-y" for you guys to be feeling this kind of . . . nervousness?'

Ivy shrugged. 'Probably. But that doesn't really matter, does it?'

'Not any more,' Sophia said, her head drooping.

Ivy gave a heavy sigh. 'I'd only *just* got used to being in the oldest grade at Franklin Grove Middle School. Now I'll have to get used to being in the *youngest* at Franklin Grove High!'

'. . . Which is way out on the border of town,' Brendan added, his shoulders hunching. 'AKA – "Next-Door to Nowhere".'

Sophia wrinkled her nose with disapproval. 'It's right next to Lincoln Vale. That means a whole bunch of kids from *out of town* – who we've never even *seen* before – will be our new classmates.'

Ivy tipped her head on to the table, her long dark hair spilling out around her. 'I am *so* not looking forward to it!'

Olivia couldn't believe it. *Ivy might wear black all the time, but her mood is never normally this dark!* 'It won't be that bad,' she said. Sitting forward, she tried to make sure her tone was confident. 'You never know. Maybe you'll love it!'

'Oh, yeah?' Ivy rolled her eyes. 'Easy for you to say, Miss I-Don't-Go-To-School-Any-More!'

Olivia blushed, shaking her head as the others joined in the gentle teasing.

'Hey, life looks pretty good for some of us,' Brendan grinned. 'If you don't even have to *go* to high school . . .'

'Private tuition *overseas*,' Sophia breathed longingly. 'In *other countries*. Starting with *England*!'

'It's just for while I'm away on set, you guys know that.' Olivia tried to sound casual, but she couldn't help feeling the excitement – and the panic – bubbling up inside her.

Finally – *finally!* – she was going to be performing again, playing the lead role in the long-delayed Big Movie Adaptation of *Eternal Sunset*! Not only was it glamorous, it was going to be the biggest acting challenge of her short career. She'd play immortal vampire identical twins who both fall in love with human – *mortal* – twin brothers. In the story, the vampire girls would seek out the reincarnated versions of their beloved humans every one hundred years, finding and falling in love with them all over again.

I hope I can pull it off, Olivia thought – not for the first time!

At least she wouldn't have any problems getting into the right emotional state. She would be acting opposite Jackson Caulfield – world-famous teen idol, fantastic actor . . . and Olivia's ex-boyfriend. She wasn't sure that all her feelings for Jackson had totally disappeared since they'd broken up earlier in the summer. Her heart still skipped a beat whenever she saw his face, even on a magazine cover. And Jackson was on the cover of a *lot* of magazines.

It's going to be great for my performance, less great for my love life.

Olivia wasn't sure how she was going to handle any of this.

'Back with Jackson again,' Sophia murmured, interrupting Olivia's thoughts. 'How cool is it that you get a second bite at the cherry?'

Olivia could feel the heat coming off her blushing cheeks. *Can Sophia actually see inside my head now?*

'The "cherry"?' Ivy snorted with laughter. 'No, it's "second bite at the *apple*".'

Sophia frowned at Ivy. 'I'm sure it's "cherry",' she said.

Ivy gave a huff of disbelief. 'And how many times have you eaten a cherry that takes *two* bites?'

'Well . . .' Sophia shrugged. 'I have to admit, you may have a point there. But cherries are better fruits anyway.'

Ivy's mouth dropped open. 'Are you crazy?' she gasped, before launching into a full-on rant about cherries, while Sophia was just as vehement on the opposing side.

Olivia traded a glance with Brendan and they both grinned ruefully, settling back to enjoy the show. Only Ivy and Sophia could get into a serious debate about the 'bite-able qualities' of cherries versus apples. Once the two of them got started, they were unstoppable.

But soon, Olivia began to tune out their voices. Honestly, she had more than enough to think about right now. Back when she'd first been cast, it had meant everything to her that she was going to star opposite the same Hollywood megastar she had met and fallen in love with right here in her hometown. What she had not realised at the time was that it couldn't last. When the film industry was hit with a strike, lots of movies were shut down – *Eternal Sunset* included. At first, Olivia had been relieved – she would have the time to properly prepare for the role, and would not have to up and leave Franklin Grove, and her family, behind.

But the strike also gave her and Jackson time to realise that they could grow apart. And they did.

Olivia had done the Hollywood scene now, and it confirmed for her where she belonged: right here in Franklin Grove. *If only Jackson had felt the same*. Her mouth twisted as she remembered their final split. As he'd toured around the world, they'd emailed less and less; their text messages had got shorter, the jokes more forced. Eventually, they both had no choice but to admit it wasn't working any more. The memory wasn't as painful as it had been but, still, she couldn't help feeling sad.

I just wish I could know for sure that we made the right decision.

Sophia's voice broke in with an all-too-painfully-relevant question: 'So, will you rekindle your romance?'

Olivia's mouth dropped open. Instinctively, she looked to Ivy for protection . . . but her twin just shrugged at her.

'We're just preparing you for the inevitable journalist questions,' she said. 'It's for your own good – think of us as your personal publicists!'

Rolling her eyes, Olivia forced herself to relax. 'I'll always be glad to know Jackson,' she said, and gave Sophia a gracious Hollywood smile.

Ivy gave her a thumbs-up of approval . . . then leapt in for a second prong of attack. 'Will you know him as *more than friends*?'

Olivia widened her smile. 'You can never have too many friends,' she said sweetly. 'And isn't the weather in England lovely? Don't you just *love* rain?'

Ivy collapsed into laughter. 'Good job,' she said. 'I like your evasiveness. It's practice for when you're being hounded by gossip columns!'

Olivia shook her head. 'I don't think that'll be any time soon. After all, this is my first starring role. I have a long way to go before I'm famous.'

'Uh-uh.' Sophia shook her head vigorously. 'Don't kid yourself, Olivia. People are already talking about you and Jackson! Everyone loves a beautiful couple, even a beautiful couple who are in splitsville.'

'*Especially* a beautiful couple who are in splitsville,' Ivy agreed. 'What could be more fascinating? The magazines will all want to know *exactly* where you two are in your relationship.'

I only wish I knew that myself! Olivia grimaced. There was so much unfinished business between her and Jackson, she couldn't even begin to

analyse it all. Even the way they'd broken up . . .
she still didn't completely understand what had
happened. She'd been even more confused
ever since Jackson had starting calling her again
lately, sounding wistful as he talked about 'the
old days'.

'Hey!' A sharp voice interrupted her musing.
It was the waitress, finally arriving. Her name-tag
said 'Joy' . . . her face said that she hadn't laughed
in at least a year. 'Are you ready to make your
orders yet? Or are you just going to hang around
chatting?'

Olivia blinked. *Wow. I guess she really isn't happy.*

Sophia smiled calmly. 'I'll have a lamb burger
with French fries, please.'

'Oh, yeah?' Brendan smirked. 'Well, I will
see your lamb burger and fries, and I will raise
you . . . a Burgel!'

Joy-the-waitress stared at him.

Brendan raised his hands as if he were

accepting applause. 'Yes, yes, that *is* a hamburger in a bagel. Traditionally eaten for breakfast, but . . . I'm feeling a little cavalier.'

As Ivy and Sophia chortled, Olivia just blinked. 'Uh . . .' She looked around the three grinning faces. 'What exactly is going on?'

'It's a new game we're playing.' Ivy dug Brendan in the ribs. 'We like to call it . . . "raising the steaks"!'

Olivia frowned. 'Raising the stakes?'

'*You* know,' Sophia said. 'Meat . . . steaks . . . and . . .' Twisting her body to hide the movement from the waitress's eyesight, she crooked her fingers in a 'fangs' gesture that definitely meant *vampires*. 'The person to order the weirdest, meatiest thing on the menu wins.'

Olivia snickered. 'Sounds . . . "fun".'

'You wanna hurry it along, folks?' Joy's face looked as sour as if she'd bitten into a lemon. 'Or am I going to grow old and die while

25

waiting for one more *wonderful* pun?'

Ivy scooped up her menu. 'I will see Brendan's Burgel and raise him a . . . um . . . er . . .'

Olivia leaned over to scour the menu at the same time as her twin. 'Wow,' she breathed. 'I can't believe it. The Burgel really is listed!'

'And it's the most ridiculous thing on there,' Ivy moaned. 'How am I supposed to top that?'

'Yes!' Brendan pumped his fist. 'I win!'

'Not so fast, Buster.' Ivy smacked down the menu with a look of triumph. 'Because *I* will have . . . a doughger!'

'A *what*?' four voices chorused at once.

Ivy beamed at the whole group. 'A hamburger,' she said, 'inside a doughnut!'

'Oh, please.' Joy rolled her eyes even as she wrote the order down. 'And for you?' She turned to Olivia, her expression weary. 'Let me guess. A hamburger in a brownie? Or in an ice-cream cone?'

26

'No, thank you.' Olivia smiled. 'I'll just have a chickpea salad.'

Joy blinked rapidly. 'Could you repeat that order, please? I don't think I got that.'

Olivia repeated it calmly, while her three vampire friends covered their mouths to keep from laughing. Joy sighed as she turned away. She stopped after a few steps, turning to call back:

'I forgot to ask. How would you kids like your burgers?'

Olivia shook her head. *As if she had to ask.*

All three vampires chorused as one: '*Rare.*'

🦇   🦇   🦇

Half an hour later, Olivia set down her spoon and looked around the table.

Ivy was lolling in her seat, clutching her stomach. 'Why didn't anybody stop me from eating that doughger?'

Brendan had his arm around Ivy and was grinning as he teased her. 'We didn't dare. You

27

and that doughger had a special thing going!'

Sophia was drawing fashion designs on her napkin with a bat-winged fountain pen. Olivia smiled around at all of them and stood, picking up her beaded purse. 'OK,' she said, giving a little wave. 'See ya.'

'Wait a minute.' Sophia dropped her pen. She turned from Olivia to Ivy and then back again, shaking her head. 'That's it? Olivia Abbott, you are going to be in *other countries* for quite some time. Is that really all you can say? "See ya"?'

'Well . . .' Olivia shrugged, still smiling.

'It has to be bigger than that!' Sophia said. 'Think of Ivy!'

Olivia looked at her twin . . . and they both burst out laughing.

'Don't worry,' Ivy said to Sophia. 'We worked this out ahead of time. We are *so* done with the big, sad, sappy goodbyes. We've had way too many of them recently.'

'We don't need them any more,' Olivia said, as she and her twin exchanged warm smiles. They had been through a lot this past year – but that had just confirmed exactly how strong their bond was.

'If there's one thing we both learned from eighth grade,' she said, 'it's that the two of us drifting apart is pretty much impossible!'

'That's right,' Ivy said. She lifted one hand in a wave. 'See you later, twin.'

Olivia was still smiling as she stepped out of the Meat and Greet a minute later. As the front door closed behind her, she cast a last look over the familiar shop fronts of Franklin Grove – the town she wouldn't be seeing for quite a while, just as Sophia had pointed out.

I really wish she hadn't said that.

Olivia took a deep breath, feeling a sudden heaviness in her chest.

This is good. It's wonderful. Because of this movie, I'm going to see the world!

But would things be different when she finally made it back?

She couldn't help it. She looked back over her shoulder . . . and found Ivy looking right at her through the diner window.

Ivy gave a little nod, just as if she had read Olivia's mind and was letting her know: *Everything's going to be OK.*

Olivia felt her shoulders slump in relief. *Ivy's always right about this kind of thing.*

With one last smile for her sister, she turned and walked quickly home. She had packing to finish and a movie to make!

Chapter Two

*B*rrrring!

The shrill sound of the alarm clock sent Ivy jerking upright. Her head hit the lid of her coffin-bed. *Ouch!* As she sat up, rubbing her head, she groaned. *Welcome to ninth grade, huh?*

It was pitch black inside the coffin-bed, but Ivy didn't need to see the clock face to know exactly what time it was: *Ridiculous O'clock!*

Any other day, she would have turned over and gone right back to sleep. Today, though . . . *Dad will just come and get me otherwise.*

She yawned and pushed the lid open. It creaked softly. She kept her eyes closed against the dawn light streaming in from her bedroom window.

Ivy hadn't thought anyone could be more nervous about her first day of high school than she was, but Mr Vega had proved her wrong. Her dad had insisted on the insanely early wake-up so that they could go over their 'plan of assimilation' before school. Worse yet, Ivy was pretty sure that he was right to be worried.

Because Franklin Grove High School was on the north edge of town, Ivy was going to meet a *lot* of new kids from Lincoln Vale, the next town over – kids who had *not* grown up with vampires in their midst! Kids who would ask questions that Franklin Grove's youngsters just didn't:

Why are these goths faster, more agile and stronger than most other boys and girls their age? Why do the goths from Franklin Grove stay *so* pale, even in summer? How can *anyone* eat a burger so *rare*?

The Franklin Grove goth kids were going to seem really, really strange to their new classmates from Lincoln Vale, and this was totally freaking out Ivy's dad. The First Law of the Night ordered that a vampire *never* revealed their true self to an outsider. But the students at Franklin Grove Middle had become so used to the odd spurt of speed or the super-quick catch of a ball that they'd stopped noticing. The same wouldn't be true at Franklin Grove High. Ivy and her friends were going to have to be extra careful . . .

'You don't want to be caught out,' her dad had warned her, his face even paler than usual. 'It could have disastrous consequences for the whole vampire community. Do you understand the seriousness of the situation?'

Oh, Ivy understood all too well. She wasn't just starting at a new school – she was putting her vampire identity on the line. Along with the extra homework, she'd need to be extra vigilant.

Ivy groaned and clambered out of her coffin, the morning light hurting her sleep-deprived eyes. *Ha.* She gave a pained laugh at the irony. *I've never felt more like a vampire than I do right now!*

She was still rubbing her bleary eyes as she padded downstairs to the kitchen. In the doorway, she stopped dead. *Am I still asleep?* She rubbed her eyes and looked again. The sight that met her eyes was the same. *No way!* She gently slapped her own face. *I have* got *to be dreaming!*

Maybe marriage had changed her dad . . . but *no way* would her father ever sit at the kitchen table in a football jersey, with a backwards baseball cap on his head!

I must be in the middle of a spectacularly strange nightmare!

'Excuse me.'

At the sound of Lillian's familiar voice behind her, Ivy sagged with relief. *Thank goodness. She'll take care of this madness!*

She turned around – and gasped.

It might have been Lillian's voice she'd heard, but it sure wasn't elegant, confident Lillian she saw before her. Instead, she saw a mouse of a woman in silly pigtails, with bookish glasses propped on her nose, textbooks tucked under one arm. As Ivy gaped in disbelief, the woman with Lillian's voice ducked her head and whispered a shy, 'Excuse me,' trying to get past Ivy into the kitchen.

'What is going on?!' Ivy's voice rose into a shriek. 'Did I wake up in Upside-Down Land? What are you two *doing*? And where did you get *props* from? And those costumes, oh my darkness – Lillian, do you even know how much Olivia would freak out if she saw those horrific sweater-vests?'

Lillian grinned and patted her textbooks as she set them down on the table. 'Think of it as a rehearsal. Your dad and I decided we should do some role-play to help you prepare for interacting with the other kids at high school.'

'And you couldn't have warned me first?' Ivy shook her head numbly as she sank down into her seat at the table. 'I can't be expected to deal with this kind of thing – I haven't even eaten my Marshmallow Platelets yet!'

'He-e-ey now!' Charles drawled. Hearing the dumb-jock tone in his usually precise voice made Ivy's head spin. 'This is deadly serious, dudette! You cannot be taken by surprise when you get there. High school can be, like, so totally, totally *lethal*!'

'Did you seriously just refer to me as "dudette"?' Ivy put one hand over her eyes. 'Please say I was imagining that. I have to have imagined that part. Or maybe I really am still asleep in my coffin.'

'*Seriously*,' Lillian repeated, 'there will be a lot of new faces. Like, a *lot*. You should definitely think about how you're going to cope with so many extra bunnies.'

'Gaah.' Ivy groaned and reached for her box of Marshmallow Platelets.

This was going to be a long morning. She needed all the help she could get.

'I'll go through with this dumb role-play if it'll make you guys happy,' she said, giving her dad and step-mom a weary look. 'But, I'm telling you, if I can cope with Charlotte Brown and her cheerleader cronies, with their perma-smiles, I can definitely cope with anything this new school throws at me.'

I think.

Suddenly, she was assailed by visions of a hallway full of perky bunnies . . . and all of their faces twisting in disgust as she walked past them. *Euch.*

Ivy swallowed hard and concentrated on pouring her Marshmallow Platelets into a bowl, while she felt both her dad and step-mom watching her like hyper-anxious hawks.

Who knew the Wallachia Academy Experience would ever feel like a fond memory?

❤   ❤   ❤

Promptly at eight a.m., Ivy was sitting outside her house, waiting for her ride to school and feeling like James Bond going undercover.

The week before, Lillian had shopped with her like a fashion master, helping her tear through the stores until they'd found the perfect *subtle* goth clothes. They were still 'Ivy' in style, but nothing that would catch the eye of Lincoln Vale bunnies as being *too* alternative. Now, she was dressed in all greys instead of blacks, from her deep grey dress, embroidered with a tasteful silver bat, to her soft, dove-grey tights. Her eyes were still lined with kohl, but she'd even changed her usual black nail polish for sparkling silver.

The one thing she had flat-out *refused* to change

was her bat ring. It had been a gift from Brendan when she'd first returned from the Wallachia Academy, and she'd never agree to take it off. *It goes where I go!*

Now Ivy twisted it nervously around her finger as she waited for the bus. For the first time in her life, Undertaker Hill didn't feel quite safe. Instead, it felt eerily silent, apart from the sound of the school bus that her vampire ears told her was only one street away. *Not long now.* It was already on its unstoppable charge towards her . . . and then it would take her all the way to school.

High school!

Just the fact that she needed *public transport* to get to school now, instead of walking, underlined how huge this day really was.

And she was doing it alone. Olivia was already on her way to London. Ivy's chest tightened at the thought. *I am going to miss her so much.*

The dull roar of a plane's engine overhead

made her head jerk up. Could that be the same plane Olivia was taking all the way to London? She narrowed her eyes. It was definitely the right timing, but was it flying in the right direction? London was due east, right? And the sun rose in the east – everyone knew that. So, if the sun was in the east, then this plane looked like it was flying north – which meant it probably wasn't her sister's plane. But then again, when Ivy and her family had last flown to Transylvania, the plane had taken off and slowly turned around, so this plane *could* have been Olivia's flight, just taking off ...

Oh, I give up, Ivy thought, as a slight headache set in. According to Charles's detailed instructions, a headache would *not* be good for the 'fiendish' educational challenge that was high school!

Then a new sound made Ivy's head jerk up. The school bus had rumbled on to Undertaker Hill. Or rather: a Yellow Monster had! From front to back, the bus blazed fluorescent yellow. It was as subtle as the sun, or a flashing neon sign that read to everyone in town: *Bunnies Aboard!*

Ivy froze as the Yellow Monster charged towards her.

I can't do this!

If only it had been black and purple, maybe she wouldn't have minded being seen getting on board . . . but this? How could any self-respecting vampire go to school in a banana on wheels?

But what choice do I have? she realised. *I'm the one who didn't want to stay at Wallachia Academy. I promised Dad that I could do this. I have to prove that he was right to let me.*

It took every ounce of pride Ivy had to force herself to her feet. Once she was there, she had to readjust her backpack just to give herself something to do . . . other than running for her life!

The bus hissed to a stop outside her house.

Its doors creaked open like the jaws of a dragon, waiting to devour her whole.

Taking a deep breath, Ivy stepped through the open doors.

The bus's driver was a middle-aged woman in a fuzzy blue sweater, and Ivy's stomach sank. Even as she smiled politely, she braced herself for the look of disdain that she knew would be aimed her way any moment now. Bunnies like this *hated* goths!

But the bus driver just smiled back at her. 'Welcome to the bus run, Ivy!' She leaned forwards, lowering her voice to a whisper. 'I know today is a big day for you, but everything will be just fine. You take it from me.' She winked encouragingly.

Ivy was so stunned, she couldn't even speak. All she could do was give the bus driver another wavering smile and then make her way down the aisle, past rows of mostly unfamiliar chattering

bunnies towards the rear bench seat where —
thank darkness! — she finally saw Sophia sitting all
by herself.

Like Ivy, Sophia had dressed down for their
first day of high school, wearing a plain black
T-shirt instead of any of her beloved rock-band
merch. Her long, dark hair was pulled back in
a tight ponytail, making her face look tense,
and her fingers and ears were bare of her usual
fashionable goth accessories.

'I'm so glad you're here!' Sophia picked up her
backpack and scooted over to make room for
Ivy. 'Is it just me, or do the streets outside look
almost . . .'

'Scary?' Ivy filled in sympathetically. 'Trust
me, it's not just you.' As she sat down next to her
friend, the bus pulled away from her house with a
rattle and jerk. Through the window, Undertaker
Hill slid past, then disappeared behind them.

Ivy took a deep breath. She didn't just feel like

she was being carried to school – she felt like she was being *pulled* along in an insistent current. *The current of change.*

And she didn't like it one bit.

Forget it, world! Ivy set her jaw hard. *No one takes Ivy Vega anywhere she doesn't want to go. I'm still in charge of my life . . . even if I am riding in a bright yellow bananamobile!*

The bus screeched to a stop, throwing everyone forwards in their seats. As Ivy pushed herself back into place, the doors hissed open and a timid figure hesitated at the entrance. Finally, she moved forwards . . . and Ivy choked as she recognised Charlotte Brown, cheerleading queen bee of Franklin Grove Middle School, looking around the bus as nervously as a baby zebra heading into a den of ravenous lions.

Charlotte's anxious gaze skittered all around the bus – then landed on Sophia and Ivy. Her face lit up into a beaming smile. 'You're here!'

She waved excitedly.

'Is she for real?' Sophia whispered, even as she half-lifted a hand to wave back.

Ivy had to bite back a laugh of astonishment. 'Well, I guess our relationship did improve a lot by the end of last year . . .'

'But still,' said Sophia, 'it's not like we've been meeting up with her over summer vacation.'

'Well . . .' Ivy hesitated as Charlotte hurried towards them. 'It's actually quite . . .' No, she had to stop there. Just thinking the word 'sweet' made her shudder.

But honestly, on a day full of danger, it didn't hurt to see how eager Charlotte was to be friendly to two of the goths she'd once despised.

'Eeee!' Charlotte squealed. She plopped herself down between Ivy and Sophia, forcing them to make space. 'I am so happy to see you guys! Are you heading for Willowton High? Please tell me you both are!'

'Sorry.' Ivy shook her head, feeling her own spirits lower. 'Franklin Grove High.'

'Oh *no*.' Charlotte slumped. 'That just sucks! And with Olivia gone, too . . .'

Ivy and Sophia traded a glance over Charlotte's head. Neither of them could have imagined a year ago that Charlotte would one day *miss* Olivia!

The bus bumped to another halt, and Olivia's friends Camilla and Holly stepped on, waving happily to Ivy and Sophia.

'At least they'll both be at Willowton,' Charlotte said, brightening. 'But it's so sad we're not all going to the same school.'

'It is,' Ivy agreed. Silently, though, she thought maybe it was a good thing that Charlotte was starting fresh in a completely new school.

At Franklin Grove Middle, Charlotte had been so used to everyone grovelling to her, it had been fatal for her personality. Now was her chance to finally make a good impression with new people

– people who weren't already impressed with her for all the wrong reasons. *She can start over*, Ivy thought, *as a nicer upgrade of herself. Charlotte 2.0.*

As the bus rumbled through town, picking up more and more unfamiliar students on the way, Ivy and Sophia both took care to practise their mundane and bunny-friendly conversation. As usual, Camilla was too focused on planning for her next movie masterpiece to notice, and Holly was too nervous to say much at all as Ivy and Sophia dragged out a tortuous conversation about popular movies, TV, and even – *gag!* – pop music. But Charlotte Brown, the bunniest bunny Ivy had ever met, noticed straight away.

'You guys!' Charlotte batted at Ivy's arm. 'I've never heard you two talk like this before.'

'Well . . .' Sophia shrugged. Her expression looked pained. 'We just thought we'd . . .'

'Expand our horizons,' Ivy finished for her, hoping she sounded like she *really* meant it.

She thought she might have turned green at the lie, but Charlotte shook her head in amazement.

'I have to tell you both, you have never been more interesting! And your clothes – they're *so* much better than they used to be. Whatever *happened* to you this summer?'

Ivy and Sophia exchanged a look of satisfaction. Their *Undercover Bunny* Operation was working perfectly. They'd just have to hope that the ruling bunnies at Franklin High were as easy to fool as Charlotte!

The bus slammed to a halt outside Franklin Grove High School, and Ivy's new-found certainty drained away. Through the window, a massive, curving cement structure spread out before them. Franklin Grove High. The windows along its sides seemed to glare at Ivy accusingly, seeing right through her carefully chosen disguise.

I'll never belong here, she thought. *Everyone will be able to tell what I really am the moment they see me.*

48

I can't fake it with all those bunnies for a whole four years!

'Come on,' Sophia whispered. Her face was pale.

Together, they followed the line of Franklin Grove High bunnies out on to the pavement. As the bus pulled away, Charlotte, Camilla and Holly all waved to them out of the rear window. Ivy's chest ached at the sight. She waved back until the bus turned the corner . . . and then they were gone.

Ivy turned to Sophia. 'We can do this,' she said.

'We can,' Sophia echoed faintly.

Neither of them moved. Together, they stared at the huge school before them. Students streamed towards it from all directions.

At least I have Sophia, Ivy reminded herself. She reached out to link arms with her friend. Together, they walked up the boulevard towards the school entrance.

Everything is going to be fine. Everything, everything, everything . . .

She had to shake her head at herself. Funny how she'd never felt *this* nervous starting at the snoot-tastic Wallachia Academy!

Franklin Grove High looked like a completely different world from Franklin Grove Middle. It was monstrously big by comparison, with lush strips of well-kept grass and flowers spread out in front of it, almost sparkling in the morning sun.

'Dad was right,' she muttered to Sophia. 'Goths would definitely stand out amid all this colour!'

Sophia only nodded. She looked too stunned to speak.

A walkway led from the front gate to the main building, lined with . . . Ivy's feet thudded to a halt as she froze in horror. *No way!*

The whole walkway was lined with non-goths – from the older grades. *Oh no*, Ivy thought. *We're going to have to walk right through a gauntlet!*

She gritted her teeth, bracing herself. 'Are you ready?' she asked Sophia.

Only silence answered her. Ivy glanced at her friend. 'Sophia?'

But Sophia wasn't paying any attention. Her eyes were fixed on a cluster of older boys halfway down the path, and her mouth had dropped open in an 'O'.

This can't be good, Ivy thought.

She narrowed her eyes, studying the group of boys. Every one of them was unfamiliar, which meant they must have come from Lincoln Vale. They all balanced on skateboards as they talked, gesturing animatedly and flipping their boards beneath their feet every few seconds to keep their balance. The tallest of them – *and, OK, the cutest*, Ivy admitted silently – was in the middle of a mime about some daredevil move he'd obviously performed on his board.

'Whoa, Finn!' The boy nearest him punched

Finn on his shoulder. 'That is, like, the raddest thing I've ever heard!'

Finn grinned goofily and did an extra flip on his skateboard – it was all the more impressive because Ivy could *not* figure out how he could see *anything* with his mop of long blond hair falling around his eyes.

Ivy shook her head. OK, so Finn was cute – in a dumb-blond sort of way – but she bet he had the exact same voice her dad had used in the kitchen this morning. *He'd just better not ever try calling me 'dudette'. Anyone who's not my dad will get an Extreme-Level Death Squint for that crime!*

Next to her, though, Sophia let out a sigh . . . and it didn't sound like disgust.

'Come on!' Ivy nudged Sophia down the path. 'Remember the Second Law,' she whispered. It was one of the most important rules of vampire society: *No falling in love with outsiders!*

'Right,' Sophia mumbled. But as they passed

the skater-boys, she let out another wistful sigh.

We might have a problem, Ivy thought grimly.

But she didn't have time to worry about it now. First, they had to get through today. *All we have to do is not draw any attention to ourselves. Easy. Right?*

Her belly tingled uncomfortably, and she gulped. *I hope that's just the doughger from yesterday. I'm not that nervous . . . am I?*

When she spotted Brendan's familiar silhouette near the main school building, she let out a sigh of pure relief. 'Finally!'

Pulling Sophia along with her, Ivy raced towards her boyfriend. He stood near the front door, and when he turned to face her, she saw that he'd dressed down too, wearing simple dark jeans and sneakers. In terms of his clothing, he wouldn't have looked out of place with the skater-boys. But he wore the expression of someone who had just seen a ghost . . . playing cards with a yeti!

'What's wrong?' Ivy asked.

He pointed a trembling finger at the school. 'I went inside. Just for a second, to check it out. It . . . It . . .'

Ivy stared at him, feeling her stomach sink. 'How bad *is* it in there?'

Brendan shook his head, his eyes wide and stunned. 'I've never seen anything like it.'

Oh no. Taking a deep breath, Ivy opened the front door. *I don't care how bright and pink and bunnified it is. I can take it, no matter what!*

Then she blinked, as the door closed behind her and her friends. *Wait a minute. Who turned out the lights?*

The foyer was a sea of darkness. And lining the corridors in every direction, propped against the lockers, lounging on the floor, and gossiping in groups, were the students of Franklin Grove High.

Ivy felt her eyes widen. The last time she had seen this many goths in one place was at a Pall Bearers concert!

Feeling dazed, she walked slowly down the first corridor, taking it all in. 'But . . .'

Her voice trailed off as a girl in ripped jeans and bone-white face paint, leaning against the wall of lockers, nodded approvingly at her T-shirt.

'Um . . . thanks?' Ivy said to the girl, trying to smile. To Brendan, though, she whispered frantically, 'Am I dreaming?'

'If you are,' Brendan croaked, 'then I am, too.'

She reached out and laced her fingers through his, hanging on for balance. They passed a group of girls sitting at the bottom of a staircase, painting each other's fingernails black. Further along the hallway, Ivy could see someone carrying a black backpack that rippled with rubber spikes.

'It's not pink,' Sophia said faintly. 'I thought it would all be pink.'

Ivy shook her head numbly. 'If any of these people saw the colour pink, they'd probably run screaming into the nearest darkened room!'

'There are more goths here than bunnies,' Brendan said. 'It's just *wrong*.'

'And look at those T-shirts.' Sophia nodded at the girls ahead of them. 'I've never even heard of some of those rock bands!'

'Whoa.' Ivy felt her legs go weak as she absorbed the truth. 'Guys,' she whispered. 'I don't think we're the outsiders at this school.'

Sophia's eyes were wide. 'Do you think . . . could it be . . .?'

Brendan nodded, looking panicked. 'I think . . . the goth kids at this high school might actually be the *in-crowd*.'

'No way,' Ivy breathed. She saw the same stunned reaction in both of her friends' eyes. But the truth was staring them in the face from all around . . . and it was wearing black.

For the first time ever, it looked like Ivy, Sophia and Brendan might actually *fit in*!

Chapter Three

I can't believe it, Olivia thought, as she bounced on her hotel bed. *I'm actually in London, England!*

A sea of dark rooftops spiked outside her window under a cloudy blue sky. In the distance, she could see Big Ben in the centre of the city. She had heard its hourly gong twice since she'd arrived and, though she knew it was just a giant clock tower, there was something . . . *magical* about a giant clock tower so far away from home.

Through the wall of her connecting room, Olivia heard her adoptive mom, Mrs Abbott, gushing down her cell phone to a friend back home. '. . . and, of course, we're determined to

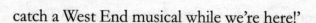

catch a West End musical while we're here!'

Olivia's adoptive dad, Mr Abbott, didn't speak, but Olivia heard a tell-tale thud as he moved to a different yoga position on the hotel room floor. Mrs Abbott might be excited about the London theatres, but Mr Abbott had spent the aeroplane ride telling Olivia all about the wonderful yoga facilities in London. Apparently, there were even outdoor yoga classes on the rooftops!

I just hope he doesn't go into a headstand too near the edge of the roof, Olivia thought, peering out the window.

She turned to pick up her guidebook. As her gaze travelled across the room, she had to blink to remind herself that she wasn't dreaming. Really, this could hardly be described as a bedroom. It felt bigger than her house in Franklin Grove! The ceiling was painted with images of famous London sites, and the opposite wall was covered with expensive electronic equipment, from a flat-screen television to a range of radios, DVD and CD players.

Hollywood stars really do *live differently!*

Taking a deep breath, Olivia opened up her guidebook and began to read. As she turned the pages, her eyes widened. *Did Mom and Dad accidentally pick up a joke version?*

Surely no one would actually call a building 'The Shard', or 'The Gherkin'. Would they? *It has to be a joke!*

There was one thing that was no joke, though. As Olivia set down the ridiculous guidebook, the luxury of her hotel room astounded her all over again. It was unbelievable. Jacob Harker, the studio executive in charge of *Eternal Sunset*, certainly went all-out when he wanted to impress the people working on his movies.

A knock sounded on the connecting door, and Mrs Abbott's head poked through. She was wearing sunglasses and had her own guidebook sticking out of her handbag. 'Hi, honey. Your dad and I want to go exploring. Are you ready?'

'Um . . .' There was a funny tingling sensation in Olivia's stomach. She put one hand on it and forced a smile. 'Why don't you guys go without me? I'm a little tired from the trip.'

'Well, if you're sure . . .' Mrs Abbot hurried across the room to press a kiss on Olivia's brow. She stroked her hair back from her face, and smiled down at Olivia. 'Get some rest, sweetheart.'

'I will,' Olivia promised. As she listened to her parents' bustling departure, she propped her shoulders against the wall and tucked the strange, fluffy 'duvet' around her, making herself a nest. It felt like she was walling herself in from the world. *I just can't face going out. Not yet.*

Between jet lag and culture shock, she had lost all sense of what time it was. The clock on the wall claimed it was early afternoon, but she felt a strange craving for cereal. *Maybe my body just doesn't want to admit that it's left America!*

It wasn't just her body that was in trouble, though. Her heart rate rocketed every time she thought about exactly where she was and exactly *who* she would be seeing on-set once the filming began. Playing two different vampire twins was going to be tough . . . but trying to act normal around Jackson was going to be Olivia's *greatest* acting challenge this summer.

A knock sounded outside, and Olivia blinked, startled out of her worries. What were her parents doing back so soon?

Then she realised: the knock hadn't come from the connecting door. It had come from the hallway outside.

As she stood up, she knew – somehow – exactly who she would find waiting for her.

Her heartbeat pulsed against her throat. There didn't seem to be enough air in the hotel room as she walked across the lush carpet. Pasting a welcoming smile on her face, she opened the door . . .

. . . and found a scruffy, unfamiliar boy standing outside, wearing baggy shorts and a jersey for some English soccer team she didn't recognise. A baseball cap was pulled down low over his face, his shoulders were slouched, and no one in the world would have had any idea who he was . . .

Except Olivia.

'Hi, Jackson,' she said softly. 'Come on in.'

Jackson Caulfield pushed up the brim of his baseball cap to give her a rueful grin, his blue eyes intense. 'You weren't even fooled for a moment, were you?'

Olivia only shook her head, smiling. But inside, she answered honestly: *I would know you anywhere.*

She couldn't say that out loud, though, could she?

Absolutely not, she told herself. If she said

that, she'd sound like she was still in love with him. He'd think she was pathetic! But now *no one* was speaking, and the silence felt like pressure building all around them, until she was ready to burst.

Olivia clasped her hands together so she wouldn't fidget. *Just say something,* she begged him silently. *Anything!*

She'd never seen Jackson looking so awkward before. He *always* knew what to say; what to do.

'So . . .' Jackson stuck his thumbs in his shorts pockets, rocking awkwardly on his heels. 'I guess . . . maybe we ought to shake hands now?'

Olivia's eyes widened in disbelief. She let out a startled laugh. 'OK . . .?' She casually held out her hand. Inside, though, she was in shock. *We were boyfriend-and-girlfriend for months. Now we're shaking hands like strangers?*

Jackson took her hand, then gave a baffled laugh. 'This is dumb, isn't it?'

'Well . . .' Biting her lip, Olivia started to step back. At the same moment, Jackson tugged on her hand, pulling her into a hug.

The unexpected move upset her balance. Olivia tipped forwards – and their noses bumped hard. 'Ow!' she yelped.

Jackson almost leaped backwards in his hurry to let her go. 'Sorry!'

Olivia stumbled back, hanging on to her aching nose and laughing nervously. 'It's OK,' she said. 'So . . . do you want to come in?' She gestured to her hotel room.

Jackson gave her the same megawatt gorgeous smile she had seen on so many movie posters and magazine covers. 'Nah.'

Ouch. Olivia couldn't stop herself from wincing. The rejection hurt even more than her bumped nose! *So much for being friends now.*

'Wait.' Jackson stepped closer, his eyes widening. 'I didn't mean it like that!'

'You didn't?' Watching him warily, Olivia lowered her hand from her nose.

Jackson sighed. Pulling off his baseball cap, he ran one hand through his thick blond hair. 'I'm such a doofus! I meant, I want to take you *out*. We still have a few more days before filming, right? And here we are in a beautiful foreign city. Don't you want to see some of it?'

Olivia glanced back through the open doorway of her hotel room to the panoramic view of London outside. 'It would be nice to see London for real instead of through plate glass,' she admitted. *And without a joke guidebook playing pranks on me!*

'But . . .' She turned back to Jackson, frowning. 'Are you sure that it's a good idea? I mean, we might not be in America any more, but we are still on *Planet Earth*. Don't you need to keep yourself well-hidden?'

Jackson's grin was wide, relieved, and even

more megawatt gorgeous than before. 'Don't worry about that part,' he said. 'Trust me. I've made us a reservation for lunch in a place where we're *guaranteed* not to be disturbed.'

🦇   🦇   🦇

An hour later, Olivia had to admit that he was right. *No one* would be able to intrude on them now, not even the most obsessed fangirl – because the lunch that Jackson was treating her to would be served in mid-air!

Ever since Olivia had spotted the London Eye on her limousine journey from the airport, she'd wanted to ride the giant Ferris wheel that stood on the edge of the River Thames. But now, as Jackson ushered her into one of the Eye's big, egg-shaped glass pods, she looked around with a combination of enchantment and confusion. *I never thought I'd see it like this!*

Inside the glass pod, an elegant table awaited them, set for two with silver that glittered in the sunlight. A light vegetarian lunch of sandwiches, wraps, hummus, pitta bread and fruits lay set out on china platters while fruit juices glimmered in crystal glasses.

A uniformed waiter bowed politely to Olivia as the door of the pod slid shut silently behind her. A second waiter hovered in the background, keeping as discreet a distance as possible in such a confined space. Outside, brightly coloured boats filled the Thames, pedestrians scurried around the streets, and the city bustled with activity while, inside the glass pod, Olivia felt the ground lift beneath her feet.

The pod gently swung into the air as the London Eye began its big circle, carrying Olivia and Jackson in an enchanted bubble.

'Well?' Jackson asked. He stood watching her, a tentative smile on his face. 'What do you think?'

'It's amazing,' Olivia said. She sat down at the table and let out a laugh as she watched the city swing past her through the rounded glass walls. 'I've never seen anything like this.'

'I know it's not exactly Franklin Grove.' Jackson grinned as he sat down across from her. 'But do you think you could get used to it?'

'Well . . .' Olivia frowned, as one of the waiters leaned over to stack her plate with food. Jackson seemed to be able to ignore the service, the way her Transylvanian grandparents could at one of their fancy banquets, but she couldn't help being aware of the waiters' presence as she spoke.

'International travel *is* exciting,' she said, 'and the movie business is, too . . . but honestly?' She leaned forwards, dropping her voice as she admitted: 'Just between the two of us, I'm already exhausted, and we haven't even *started* filming yet. I don't know how you put yourself through this so many times a year!'

Jackson nodded, looking sympathetic. 'Honestly? I'm not sure, either. But . . .' He shrugged, picking up an avocado wrap from his plate. 'I've already got more projects lined up, so I can't let myself worry too much about it.'

'That's right!' Olivia beamed. 'I just heard you got that role as the teenage super spy! That sounds fantastic!'

Jackson stared at her, his wrap frozen halfway to his mouth. 'Did you see that in *Teen Talk*?'

'Um . . .' Olivia's mouth went dry. She couldn't tell him the truth – that she'd read it in *VAMP* magazine! 'I think . . . I don't remember,' she mumbled, wincing.

Jackson shook his head, looking disgusted. 'Don't believe anything you read in *Teen Talk*. Seriously. They're hardly the high standard of journalism, even by celebrity journalism standards.'

Olivia forced herself to chew endlessly on a single piece of lettuce, cursing herself. *Why did I have to say anything about it in the first place?*

VAMP Magazine was far more credible than

Teen Talk, but it was also a secret kept by the vampire community. And even if it hadn't been, she couldn't bring herself to admit that she'd been reading *any* celebrity gossip articles about him. If she did, she'd come off as a gullible fangirl.

Or worse: she might even seem like the kind of stalker ex-girlfriend she'd seen on TV shows, obsessed with him in some unhealthy way!

'It wasn't *Teen Talk,*' she mumbled.

'No?' Jackson frowned. 'Where was it, then? I didn't think anyone else had reported it.'

'Um . . .' Caught, with both the waiters' gazes on her, Olivia swallowed hard. 'Maybe . . . I might have seen it in the *New York Times*?'

Jackson choked on his wrap. 'Are you serious?' he managed, in between coughs.

Olivia licked her lips nervously. 'I . . . think so?'

'Wow.' He shook his head as he finally stopped coughing. 'I can't believe it. I thought the only

71

time my name *ever* got mentioned in the *Times* was when their film critic trashed my performance in *The Groves*. He said I was wooden.'

'*What?*' Olivia gasped in outrage. 'Who would say that? That's ridiculous! It's just not true. You were fantastic! You totally –' *Oops.* She snapped her mouth shut too late, wincing. *D'oh!* 'Um . . . not that I'm a stalker fangirl,' she muttered, her cheeks burning. 'Obviously.'

'Are you sure about that?' Jackson raised his eyebrows. 'You've apparently been reading all about me –'

'In the *Times*!' Olivia yelped. 'I was just reading the film section!'

But he was already laughing, his blue eyes bright with amusement. 'Don't worry! I get it. I would have read articles about you, too.'

Olivia blinked. 'You would have?'

'Of course.' He shrugged, as if it were obvious. 'Anyway, I shouldn't be teasing you like this.' His gaze dropped to his plate. 'Especially not now. See, I've got something very important and a little . . .' He gave an awkward laugh. '. . . well, it's a little embarrassing, to tell the truth. But I really want to talk to you about it.'

'OK . . .' Olivia felt a flutter of nervousness clutch at her throat. She could sense the waiters trying not to listen.

Was Jackson really about to talk about . . . *them*? As a couple? If he wanted to re-open that chapter of their lives . . .

Her breathing stopped as Jackson reached across the table and took her right hand. His fingers felt warm and strong and achingly familiar.

'Olivia,' he said. His voice throbbed with emotion. 'I really, really need . . .' He hesitated, looking anguished.

'Yes?' Olivia's voice came out as a squeak. Her left hand was clutched so tightly around her napkin, it would have shredded if it hadn't been made of cloth.

'. . . your help,' he finished in a rush. Then he let out a whoosh of breath and rolled out his shoulders. 'Whew.' He gave her a lopsided grin. 'It was hard to get that out!'

Olivia just stared at him, her mouth hanging open. Outside, the sights of London swung past, exotic and beautiful, and having no effect on her because, inside, she felt numb. 'What are you talking about?' she asked faintly.

'It's the role. I mean, *roles*.' Grimacing, Jackson sat back. 'For our London scenes, I have to do English accents for the brothers.'

'Yeah . . .?' Her head was still whirling with reaction as she drew her hand away from his.

He didn't seem to notice. 'Well, one of the brothers is "posh" – upper-class English. I can do that, no problem! But the other brother . . .' Jackson sighed. 'He's a "Cockney", a real working-class Londoner, and I just can't get that

74

accent right.'

'And you think *I* can?' Olivia shook her head, almost laughing. 'Jackson, look at me. I've never even been to England before!'

'But you're awesome at voices, though,' Jackson said. 'Your robot voice in Camilla's sci-fi version of *Romeo and Juliet* was amazing!'

It was *amazing*, Olivia thought wistfully. But she wasn't thinking of the strange voice Camilla had made her put on. She was thinking of that opening night performance, when Jackson as Romeo had given her a very first kiss . . .

Focus! She jerked herself out of the memory and found Jackson looking at her expectantly:

'So, can you help me?'

'Well . . .' Was it really a good idea to spend so much one-on-one time with Jackson, when her feelings were so confused? Olivia hesitated. 'Don't you have a voice coach?'

'Of course.' Jackson made a face.

'Unfortunately, we don't really see eye-to-eye.'

'Hmm.' *Just think of it as work!* Olivia told herself firmly. She sat up straighter, trying to look professional and confident, and scooped up a strawberry from the bowl of fruit. 'All right, then. Why don't you try a Cockney voice for me now?' She smiled brightly and popped the strawberry into her mouth. 'How bad can it be?'

'OK.' Jackson took a deep breath. 'Awight, gawvanah – there's sumwan arskin' for ya on the doggonbone.'

'Um . . .' Olivia's eyes widened as she almost choked on the fruit. She noticed one of the waiters raise his eyebrows to the other. 'OK. I have to admit, I have no idea if that was a good accent or not. But I'm pretty sure that whatever you just said, it wasn't in English!'

Jackson grinned, visibly relaxing. 'It's pretty different, anyway. But I really need to practise without my vocal coach glaring at me the whole time. So . . .' He looked at her hopefully. 'What do you think? Will you help me? I don't want the whole of England laughing at me when I open my mouth on-screen!'

Olivia pressed her lips together, forcing herself to stop and think it through before she answered. What would Ivy say, if she were here?

OK, I think I know the answer to that one. Fiercely protective Ivy would not let Olivia put herself in a situation where she could be hurt again.

But on the other hand . . . Olivia wanted the movie to be good, didn't she? And she didn't want *anyone* laughing at Jackson. He may not have been her boyfriend any more, but that didn't mean she'd stopped caring about his feelings. And if helping him out meant spending lots of time together . . .

That's what I want, she realised. *Whether it's sensible or not!* She'd been so nervous about seeing Jackson again, but the last hour had actually been wonderful. When they'd broken up, her only hope was that they would manage to be civil, but this had been *way* more than civil. Olivia had almost forgotten just how much fun it was to be with him!

And what is Ivy going to say about that? She smiled ruefully, imagining her twin's reaction.

'OK,' she said to Jackson. 'I'll do it.'

'Yes!' He pumped one fist in victory. 'Thank you so much. You're really saving me!'

Olivia laughed and picked up another strawberry. 'I don't know about that, but I do have an idea. You want to get your accent right, don't you?'

'Of course.' He frowned. 'So?'

'So, why don't we *both* adopt disguises?' she said. 'Then we can go out and walk among real Londoners, instead of just relying on your vocal coach and her rules. We can listen to how people *really* talk, to get the rhythms of the speech down.'

'Olivia Abbott, you are brilliant.' Jackson beamed at her as he picked up a last sandwich. 'Why don't we try it later today?'

'Sounds good to me,' Olivia agreed. She smiled to herself as the pod carried them slowly back down to earth.

So much for having a quiet, lazy afternoon . . . but this has definitely *been a lunch to remember!*

Chapter Four

Even lunchtime is a bizarre experience! Ivy thought. She stared down at her food, but couldn't bring herself to eat it. She was too busy reeling from the shock revelations of the morning.

Not only was Franklin Grove High full of goths, they seemed to be the largest demographic – the most popular social group! Even Mr Russell, Ivy's English teacher, had been wearing a long-sleeved black Tee underneath his collared shirt. More than that, he'd used a Destroy the Dream Boat track to inspire a creative writing session!

When Ivy had had to stand up and introduce

herself, she'd received a round of applause before she'd even opened her mouth. When she'd sat back down afterwards, the girl sitting next to her had whispered, 'How do you get to be so cool?'

Ivy was lost for words – and that *never* happened.

Now, she was in the school cafeteria, with a burger in front of her, surrounded by a sea of goths. They filled up the prime table in the cafeteria, just by the dessert bar and next to the doors that opened up on to the courtyard outside. Posters for Ivy's favourite bands hung on the cafeteria walls, and a sign over the dessert bar announced their 'Dark Special' – a dark chocolate cheesecake, with tiny bats drawn perfectly in icing.

And if all that wasn't weird enough, Ivy could see a group of blonde, tanned 'bunny' girls sat in a dark corner, pressed uncomfortably into a too-small table. But they sure weren't acting like any bunnies she'd ever seen before.

Back at Franklin Grove Middle, those bunny
girls would have been confidently chatting and
laughing, well aware that they ruled the whole
school. Here, though, they sat hunched and
whispering, darting nervous looks over their
shoulders whenever one of them made too
much noise.

Between the prime table of goths and the back
corner of bunnies, like a buffer zone, was a table
of . . . well, *regulars* was all that Ivy could think to
call them. And she couldn't believe it. The regular
kids had a better table than the bunnies!

Sighing, she turned back to her own table. The
leader of the goths, a girl in junior year called
Amelia Thompson, was in the middle of a lecture
that made the younger students at the table lean
forwards to catch every single word. Ivy had
realised that Amelia was Queen Bee of this group
as soon as everyone had crowded around her
in the cafeteria line, asking her opinion on what

was the right lunch to eat on a Monday.

I never knew that goths could have Queen Bees, Ivy thought glumly, as she looked around the pale, rapt faces. *Just one more thing I was wrong about!*

Amelia was an absolute blueprint for everything a goth should be, from the silver rings in the braided strands of her hair to the heavy black boots, the pale skin and the little kilt she was wearing. It was all Classic Goth – and she clearly knew it. Ivy listened in disbelief as Amelia lectured those around her:

'Goths never, *ever* tan, so don't get careless just because it's turning into fall. Just because there are clouds doesn't mean that you're safe. Don't *ever* go out without sunblock!' Smiling, she pulled out a tube from her black shoulder bag. 'Personally, I like SPF50, for maximum protection. I even put it on when it's raining!'

Speechless, Ivy could only stare. *Is she for real?*

'Now, as for clothing . . .' Amelia leaned

forwards, her expression turning intent. 'You should all have at least three shades of black in your wardrobe – matt black, faded black and grey-black.'

The girl across from Ivy pulled out a notepad and started scribbling notes, looking panicked. All around the table, Ivy could see goths studying their own clothes with worried expressions. *They're probably trying to figure out if they're wearing matt black or faded black!* Ivy rolled her eyes, fighting back a snicker.

But Amelia's next words made her blood run cold.

'Most of all, I cannot overstate just *how* important it is to avoid associating with non-goths.' Amelia looked grimly around the table, holding each person's gaze in turn. She tried to catch Ivy's eye, but Ivy had developed a sudden and urgent interest in her food tray. 'Maybe you'll be tempted. Maybe some will seem OK. But a true goth will never fall for that trap!'

What?! Ivy's mouth fell open. This was going way too far.

Ivy had always loved being a true goth herself, but she would *never* dictate to anyone else how they should dress or behave. Being a Goth was all about creativity and imagination, not falling into line! And no friendships with non-goths? By those rules, Ivy shouldn't have anything to do with her own sister, one of the kindest human beings she knew!

No way am I following that *rule*, she thought grimly. *If Amelia thinks she can tell me what to do, she can —*

Brendan nudged her elbow, and Ivy shook herself, making sure a death-squint did not come over her face. She met his eye and could read the expression on his face straight away: *Don't let them see what you're thinking*.

This was Ivy's first day at a new school. She

didn't want to make enemies – not yet. It wouldn't be fair to Brendan or Sophia to draw the fire of the most popular girl in school.

And it's sure not happening so far. Ivy's mouth twisted. Amelia had announced at the beginning of lunch that Ivy would be sitting on her left. At the time, Ivy had shrugged and agreed, not realising exactly what an 'honour' it was supposed to be. Now, she could feel admiring glances aimed her way from all around the cafeteria. They made her hunch her shoulders with irritation.

These people really are crazy. I'm not supposed to be popular!

Beside her, Amelia had launched into her opinions of the Pall Bearers' latest album, Ivy's favourite. *At least we can agree on one thing,* Ivy thought. *We both know that the Pall Bearers totally suck, in the best way possible!*

As if she'd heard Ivy's thought, Amelia shot her a sudden look. 'That's *it*!' she said. 'That's why you seemed so familiar. You're that girl who got up on stage and sang at their summer show in Franklin Grove!'

'What?' Ivy frowned. 'I didn't –'

'You didn't realise anyone would *remember*?' said Brendan, grabbing her left hand under the table and squeezing.

Sophia reached over to grab her other hand. 'How could *anyone* forget something so *memorable*?' she asked firmly.

Ivy stared at them both. 'But –'

'Yup, that was Ivy,' Brendan told Amelia. 'She was picked right out of the crowd.'

Ohhh! Now Ivy remembered. Olivia had gone to the concert disguised as Ivy to use Ivy's set of free tickets, as a favour to Brendan and Sophia while Ivy was at school in Transylvania. Unfortunately for Olivia, she'd been chosen at random to sing in front of the audience. She'd been photographed in her

Ivy-guise, desperately trying to look comfortable while singing the words 'I hate you' in front of thousands of goths!

Poor Olivia. Ivy bit back a laugh at the thought of her prim, pink-loving sister in that situation. The fact that they were identical twins could be useful . . . but their twin-switches did sometimes get them both into trouble!

'That's right,' Ivy said, gathering herself. 'That was me. I sang with the Pall Bearers.'

Amelia stared at her, her expression suddenly open and vulnerable. 'Was it amazing?'

'It was . . . awesome,' Ivy muttered, and picked up her burger to hide her expression.

At least that wasn't much of a lie. It really *would* have been awesome, if only she hadn't been trapped at Wallachia Academy!

She had never been so glad to hear the bell signalling the end of lunch. The moment it sounded, she leapt to her feet, carrying her tray –

and collided hard with a blonde bunny in a baby pink mini-dress. Ivy's tray tilted and spilled edible carnage all over her deep grey dress.

'Oh no!' The bunny girl gasped, jumping backwards. She clapped one hand to her mouth and stared at Ivy with stricken eyes. 'I'm so sorry. I didn't mean to! It was an accident!'

'Don't worry about it.' Ivy shrugged. 'It was my fault. I wasn't looking where I was going.'

The bunny girl gave a squeak of panic and took another step backwards. 'No, no, no. I didn't say that! I never said that!' She swallowed hard, pulling out her wallet and handing it to Ivy with trembling fingers. 'I'll reimburse you for any damage to your clothes, I promise. Please –'

'Don't be silly.' Ivy gently pushed the wallet away. 'It was *my* fault, remember?'

'No, it *wasn't* your fault. Please!' There were beads of sweat popping up on the bunny girl's forehead now, as she darted a look at the table of watching goths. 'Let me buy you lunch tomorrow.'

Ivy winced. 'You really don't have to do that.'

'Yes, I do. I really do.' She forced a five-dollar bill into Ivy's hands. 'Please, just *take it*!' With a wail of panic, she turned and fled for the door.

Ivy stared at the crumpled bill in her fingers and shook her head helplessly. She couldn't wait to get out of the crowded cafeteria. The moment she'd finished clearing up the mess, she hurried out with Sophia and Brendan on either side. Once they were safely out of hearing range of the others, she hissed, 'This is ridiculous! I thought being the new girl would be difficult, but I had no idea being a bunny would be even harder! What is *wrong* with this school?'

Sophia just shook her head, looking shell-shocked.

Brendan sighed. 'It's different, that's for sure.'

Ivy gritted her teeth. 'The ceilings might as well be the floors. It's *that* upside down. I don't like –'

'Hey, wait up!' It was Amelia, calling out behind them as she stepped out of the cafeteria, surrounded by a group of black-clad girls.

Ivy sighed as she watched the group move. Amelia strode forward confidently, but every girl around her did a funny kind of crab-walk, keeping one eye on Amelia with every step, and trying to copy her every move. Maybe they were trying to do it without looking super-obvious . . . but as it was, it was still *very* noticeable.

With both eyes on Amelia, the girl beside her walked straight into a locker. *Crash!*

Ivy cringed, but Amelia didn't even look around at the noise. She aimed straight at Ivy, forcing Sophia to step aside. 'Well done!' She tucked her hand into Ivy's arm, lowering her voice confidentially. 'I saw how you handled that tricky situation in the cafeteria. Bunnies have a tendency to turn up at the most unwelcome moments, don't they?'

'Uh . . .' Speechless, Ivy tried to edge away, but there was no room.

'You were very gracious about it,' Amelia said. 'I'm impressed. You chose not to give that silly girl a hard time, even though she deserved it.'

'What?' Ivy spluttered. 'It was an accident! It could have happened to anyone.'

Amelia smiled thinly. 'Trust me, you don't have to cover for her.'

'I'm not "covering" for anyone.' Ivy gritted her teeth. 'Why would it matter? It's not important.'

'You see how good she is?' Amelia glanced back at her admirers. 'She's so cool, she doesn't even have to bother giving bunnies a putdown!' She gave Ivy a wink as she squeezed her arm, then released it. 'Don't worry. You and I both know what the truth is.'

'Uh . . . uhhhhrgh . . .' Ivy opened and closed her mouth like a fish as Amelia sauntered off down the hallway, followed by her group of admirers, who kept one eye on her and the other on the lockers.

Ivy swung round to her friends. 'Did that just happen?' she demanded.

Sophia shook her head, her eyes glazed with shock. 'This school . . .'

Brendan said nothing.

Together, they turned to walk towards history class . . . and bunnies scattered all around them, crashing into each other in their desperation to make space for the three goths.

Ivy felt sick as she finally realised the truth. *It's bad enough that the goths are the popular crowd at Franklin Grove High . . . but are they the bullies as well?*

🦇   🦇   🦇

Whew. We finally made it here! Olivia let out a sigh of relief as she stepped on to a crowded London street with Jackson by her side. It had taken serious convincing to talk her parents into letting her wander the streets of London in disguise with

Jackson, and she wasn't sure which they were more worried about: her physical safety in the big foreign city, or her emotions from spending so much time with her famous ex-boyfriend!

They had finally made it out of the hotel, though, with Olivia's long brown hair pinned up beneath a floppy hat, her blue eyes hidden behind heart-shaped sunglasses. She had her cell phone tucked safely in the pocket of a freshly-bought pair of baggy, shapeless jeans from a store just down the road.

Her parents had finally relented when she'd convinced them that the trip was 'essential' research for the movie – but even then, they'd only agreed on the condition that she call them every fifteen minutes and be back at eight-thirty p.m. She'd never had such an early curfew back home!

They were a world away from Franklin Grove, though, as they walked into the vibrant, colourful Borough Market. Stalls rose up on every side, selling everything from fruits and vegetables to French patés, goggle-eyed fish and Indian curries. The voices of the traders echoed all around the market, calling out to passers-by.

They might as well have been speaking a foreign language, for all that Olivia could understand!

'Watch out, mate, ya nearly knocked me off me plates!'

'I'm not trying to rob ya of your bees . . .'

'Get on the dog to yer trouble. She'll sort ya right out!'

'Yer bees are safe with me!'

Olivia's head whirled. She whispered to Jackson: 'Do people in London actually own so many bees that they have to worry about people *stealing* them? And, do they actually have bees *on* them – like, in their coat pockets, or something? Won't they get stung?'

Jackson grinned underneath the shade of his baseball cap. 'Think about it. "Bees and honey" . . . rhymes *with . . .?'

'Money!' Olivia gasped. 'That makes so much more sense.'

'Yup. Just like *dog* means *phone*,' Jackson explained. 'Because "phone" rhymes with "dog and bone". It's called Cockney rhyming slang.'

Olivia looked around the market with fresh eyes. 'I don't know how anyone can have a normal conversation in this city!'

'Now you know why I've been having trouble.' Jackson smiled. 'I was hoping to learn an accent, not a whole second language!'

Olivia couldn't help but laugh – until she felt his hand take hers. For a moment she stopped breathing, even as her fingers instinctively returned the pressure that came from his. The feeling of their hands together was so familiar and right, it was almost painful.

It doesn't mean anything, she told herself. *He's just trying to make it easier to guide me through this crowd.* With so many people shoving for position, holding hands was the only way Jackson could make sure they didn't lose each other in the crush.

It still feels romantic, though, she admitted to herself.

'Oh no,' Jackson groaned. 'They're here!'

Olivia looked around, but she didn't recognise anyone in the sea of faces. 'Who? Where?'

'Hurry!' Jackson pulled her with him through the crowd and down a narrow side street.

As the sounds of the noisy market receded, Olivia heard a dull, two-tone alarm sound going off nearby. Without stopping, Jackson dug his phone out of his pocket. It was flashing red.

'We've been spotted,' Jackson said. His face was grim. 'It's one of those JacksonWatch websites.'

'Oh no.' Olivia grimaced. Those sites weren't just innocent fanpages – they tracked Jackson's every move. 'I thought you had Amy feeding them false information,' she said.

Jackson's manager, Amy Teller, was fiercely protective of her client, and usually ran interference so that he was only looking over his shoulder twenty-two hours a day.

'Sometimes, they still get it right.' Jackson shrugged. 'Amy had my phone company hook up my cell, though, so I get alerted any time one of the sites has good info. I guess today they do.'

Instinctively, Olivia tightened her grip on his hand. 'What now? Should we turn back and try to disappear into the crowd at the market?'

Jackson looked back and sighed. 'Too late.'

When Olivia followed his gaze, she saw a cluster of teenage girls gathered at the top of the side street. All of them had their smartphones out, and they were whispering to each other as they looked around with narrow-eyed, predatory gazes.

They're like vultures, Olivia thought, *hunting for fresh meat!* She knew that she should have been feeling tension and dread, but she wasn't. She had to bite back a nervous giggle when she realised – here she was, in a romantic foreign city, in her very own caper. It was the most exciting thing that had ever happened to her . . .

. . . *And considering that my family is vampire royalty,* she thought, *that is saying something!*

One of the girls let out a yelp as a tanned man wearing sunglasses walked past them. 'Isn't that the singer who's going out with that soap star?'

Jackson squeezed Olivia's hand. When she looked at him, she could see a rueful smile on his face – it may have been a weird, scary situation, but he looked like he was seeing the funny side. 'Come on,' he said, 'while they're distracted.'

Olivia ran with him down the side street, struggling to keep up. He pulled her around a corner . . . and then stopped dead.

They'd come to an embankment overlooking the Thames. The river stretched before them, the sun was setting over London, and it would have looked dreamily romantic . . . if only it hadn't been for the swell of a scream rising behind them.

They'd been spotted.

Olivia glanced back and echoed Jackson's groan. A new group of teenage girls was thundering towards them.

'Jackson!'

'It's really him!'

'Wait for meeeee!'

Still looking over her shoulder, Olivia nearly fell when Jackson yanked her forwards, dragging her to one side and then through a narrow doorway.

'I've got an idea! Keep a lookout,' he hissed. 'Tell me if any of them see us here.'

Olivia crossed her arms like a bouncer and kept watch through the doorway. Behind her, she could hear Jackson in a whispered conversation with someone. '. . . if you can just help us . . .' she heard, along with, 'it's her *favourite* play . . .' The girls were at the far end of the street, peering down into the passing boats as if they thought Jackson might have jumped into one of them.

Olivia felt Jackson's hand close firmly on to her arm as she was pulled backwards through another doorway, into an open-aired space crammed full of people. Men and women stood pressed together all around, but no one moved. No one spoke. All their eyes were fixed on something behind Olivia's back.

Then a voice spoke, uttering words Olivia knew very well:

'Two of the fairest stars in all the heaven,
'Having some business, do entreat her eyes . . .'

Slowly, Olivia turned to face the stage.

There was a patch of purple-blue above their heads – a circular gap in the roof of the theatre invited the evening sky in. Tiers of seats rose in a semicircle around a stage, where actors in Elizabethan dress performed a scene she knew only too well: the famous 'balcony scene', where Romeo first courts Juliet.

Olivia knew exactly where they were, now. It had to be the famous, open-air Globe Theatre, where Shakespeare himself had performed. The conversation she'd half-overheard must have been Jackson talking to a doorman, bartering for late entrance to the show – a play that they had acted in together at school . . .

. . . where they had shared their first kiss.

I can't be here, Olivia thought, as Romeo and Juliet fell in love on stage. *I can't pretend we're just friends while we watch this!*

But there was no way out. The standing-room audience was pressed tightly around her. And even if she got out, Jackson's fans were stalking the streets outside the theatre.

Jackson took her hand as the balcony scene

continued. His voice echoed Romeo's words, whispering them under his breath:

'O, that I were a glove upon that hand

'That I might touch that cheek!'

Olivia swallowed hard, fighting down emotion as his hand pressed against hers. Yes, she and Jackson had performed together in this play, but could he really have *known* that this was her favourite piece of Shakespeare's writing? Or was that an excuse to get them in? *If he does*, she thought, *he knows me better than I realised.*

Heads were turning, as other audience members shot Jackson annoyed looks because he was 'talking'. Jackson didn't even seem to see the other audience members, though. His face was rapt with emotion as he gazed at the stage . . . and held Olivia's hand.

When it was time for Juliet's monologue, Olivia found herself torn.

Should I give him back the lines?

She still knew the play by heart. How could she forget? On the other hand, she didn't want to annoy any more theatre-goers. She nibbled on her lip, hesitating.

Then Jackson turned to look directly at her as he whispered along with another line:

'*I know not how to tell thee who I am . . .*'

Olivia froze, caught by the emotion in his eyes.

Was he only caught up by the play? Or did those words have any extra meaning for him?

If she hadn't been in the middle of a theatre audience that was gripped in absolute, respectful silence, Olivia could have screamed!

I don't know what to do!

If this strange day had taught her anything, it was that she had been lying to herself about her feelings. She had never really fallen out of love with Jackson. The realisation hit her like a thunderbolt. *Maybe I never will.*

But she still lived in Franklin Grove. He still

travelled from movie set to movie set. None of the issues that had split them apart had changed.

They might still seem perfect for each other . . . but could it ever *really* work?

Chapter Five

As soon as Ivy arrived at the park in Lincoln Vale, she saw Brendan waiting for her, his hands clasped tightly.

'What's wrong?' She hurried across the grass, fighting panic. Ever since she'd got his text message after school, she'd been worried – and judging by the nervous look on her boyfriend's face, she had been right to feel that way.

As he stood at the edge of the park, Brendan's face looked even more pale than normal, and his expression was tense as he pointed over his shoulder. 'See for yourself,' he said.

Frowning, Ivy followed the direction of his

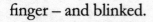

finger – and blinked.

'Wait a minute,' she said. 'Is that Sophia?'

Of all the people she'd never expected to see hanging out in a Lincoln Vale park, Sophia was probably top of the list! Ivy's best friend was lounging just beside the purpose-built skatepark with her head tipped back, wearing sunglasses and . . .

Ivy's jaw dropped open. 'Is she *tanning*?' Everyone knew how bad the sun was for vampires!

Brendan turned up his hands in a *Who knows?* gesture. 'Or she's pretending to.'

'Well . . .' Ivy gulped. 'That's *one* way to make sure no one realises you're a vampire. But we need to figure out what's going on!'

She started towards the crowded skatepark. *Time for an extraction operation, stat!* But as she set off towards her friend, students began crowding around her.

'Ivy?'

'Oh, wow, it's Ivy!'

Oh no, she thought. *The popularity's kicking in again.* How did celebrities deal with this All. The. Time? It was exhausting – and *inconvenient*.

Near-goths and bunnies came streaming across the park to join her.

'I've been wanting so badly to meet you!'

'You're *Amelia's* friend, aren't you?'

'No!' Ivy said. She had to step back as two intense-looking goths descended on her, looking as hungry as if she were an afternoon snack. 'Not really,' she said, trying to walk past them. 'I just met Amelia today.'

'But I saw you *talking* to her.' One of the goths, whose hair was a bright magenta, sighed wistfully as she blocked Ivy's escape route. 'Amelia actually *spoke* to you! And you got to speak back!'

'Uh . . .' Ivy blinked. 'Yeah, so?'

The goth-girls let out a moan of envy. 'You are

so cool!' Over her shoulder, Ivy could just glimpse Sophia – but her friend may as well have been on the opposite side of a huge ravine. How was she ever going to get to her?

Argh! Ivy looked for an escape route, but there was no way out – and more ninth-graders were flocking towards her from all around the park. *I never realised being popular was so hard!* These wannabe groupies were sticking to her like the wedding confetti she was still finding in her hair!

Maybe it's time for a death-squint, she thought. *That would chase them all away!* But as she looked into the hopelessly adoring faces, she felt guilt twisting inside her. They didn't mean any harm. They were just *in her way*.

Luckily, Brendan stepped in front of her, and put his hand flat out, like a celebrity's no-nonsense bodyguard. 'OK, guys.' His voice was firm. 'We want some time alone, now. Got it?' He took hold of Ivy's hand and she heard some of the girls give audible sighs of adoration. One of them whispered in her friend's ear and Ivy caught the words 'so sweet' and 'adorable'.

'If *you* say so, Brendan,' said one of the bunnies. 'We'll leave you to it.'

'See you soon, Ivy,' said Magenta Hair. 'Maybe with Amelia, too, next time? Right?'

Ivy let out a yelp as the last of her followers drifted obediently away. 'The sooner we can get out of this park, the better!' She stomped across the grass to Sophia's lounging figure. She still had her face turned to the sun, ignoring the crowded skatepark beside them. 'What are you doing?' she hissed.

Sophia jerked upright. Her sunglasses slid down her nose and her backpack tipped over, spilling its contents on to the skatepark pavement. 'Ivy? What are you . . .?'

'I could ask you the same thing,' Ivy said. 'I mean – wait!' She gasped. '*I don't believe it.*' She pointed at where Sophia's backpack was spilling on to the pavement. 'Is that *gingham*?'

'No!' Sophia scrambled to stuff the very-much-gingham fabric back into the backpack. 'That's just . . . for a project.'

'*What* project?' Ivy demanded. 'We're in all the same classes. I would *know* if you had a gingham-y assignment. What is up with you?'

'Nothing!' Sophia shoved her sunglasses back into place, hiding her eyes. 'I was just . . . looking to meet some of the people from Lincoln Vale. If we're going to be at school with them, it's probably a good idea to make friends, right? So they don't suspect anything?'

'Hmm.' Ivy crossed her arms. '*I'm* already starting to suspect something!'

Before she could continue, though, shouts of excitement sounded behind her. A skateboard whizzed by so close, she could feel the breeze against her back. She spun around.

111

Finn the skater-boy was bowing to the crowd, his blond hair windblown and his grin wide and happy. His buddies gathered around to pound his back and bump his fist.

'Bodacious "full cab", brah!'

'You are the "See-sen"!'

'You mean "*Sensei*", doofus!'

As she watched the skaters joke with each other, Ivy looked beyond them and saw girls in matching pale blonde, pixie-style haircuts. Skater-girls. They were cheering and applauding. 'Go Finn!'

Ivy rolled her eyes. *I can't believe anyone could get that excited about a few flips on a skateboard!* Turning her back on the skaters, she focused on what was important.

'You know how I make friends?' she said to Sophia. 'I ask them questions, and they give me answers. Some people call that "conversation".'

'Yeah,' Brendan put in. 'You not making

conversation is like a world-class baseball . . . thrower man not using his "wicked arm" . . .'

Ivy sniggered, giving Sophia a playful nudge. 'See how odd you're being – Brendan's trying to make *sports* references.'

Sophia looked down, her fingers twisting through the strap of her backpack. 'I . . . well, I didn't . . .' she stammered, then sighed. 'I just became shy once I got here.'

'You? Shy?' Ivy shook her head in disbelief as Brendan gave a soft laugh. 'OK, I was just joking before, but now I'm a bit worried – something weird is *definitely* going on here.'

When Sophia didn't answer, Ivy gave a frown. 'Look, let's just go, OK?' She scooped up Sophia's backpack. 'We can . . . Oh. My. *Darkness*.' Her jaw dropped open as she saw what was revealed underneath. 'Did you . . .' her voice spiralled upwards in shock '. . . actually *buy* a skateboard?'

Sophia hid her face in her hands.

Ivy looked at Brendan, who just looked back at her with wide, stunned eyes. Then she looked back down at the skateboard. It was bright orange, and even more fluorescent than their school bus! '*Why?*' she asked faintly.

Sophia shrugged. 'I just . . . wanted to give it a *try*, that's all. It looked like fun.'

'But why did you come here?' Brendan's eyes narrowed suspiciously. 'Why not skate in Franklin Grove?'

Sophia crossed her arms. 'This is where the skaters hang out. Where better to learn?'

Ivy frowned. There was something in her friend's voice. Something defensive . . . 'Are you sure that's the only reason?'

'Of course it is! It was safer for me to practise here.' Sophia lifted her chin. 'If I'd tried in Franklin Grove, and failed, everyone I know would have *seen* me. It would have been too embarrassing.' She stared Ivy full in the face, though it was difficult to see exactly what her expression was, behind those sunglasses.

Ivy was about to respond, when a chorus of *'Cool!'* behind her cut her off. She turned and saw the skater-girls applauding Finn, who had probably just done another fancy move with a silly name. Ivy shook her head. *Only 'cool' this time? What happened to 'bodacious'?*

She snorted. *Maybe Finn's getting over-the-hill already.* But when she turned back round, Sophia was watching Finn intently from behind her sunglasses . . . and her mouth had formed into the same admiring O-shape that Ivy could see on the gingham-ified girls who were applauding the older blond boy.

That's it . . .

Ivy nodded to herself. It wasn't going to do her best friend any good to sit off to the side, making 'goo-goo' eyes at an older boy who didn't notice her. If they weren't careful, this shyness

– so *un*-Sophia – might become permanent. And Ivy had seen enough of High School this week to know that it would be even tougher to handle if Sophia kept herself to herself too much. *A healthy serving of 'tough love' coming right up*, she thought.

'You know, Sophia,' said Ivy. 'If you want to learn to skate, you should go for it.' She stepped aside, clearing Sophia a path to the skatepark. 'Right now!'

Sophia scooted backwards, clutching her board to her chest. 'What?'

'Come on. That's why you're here, isn't it?' Ivy raised her eyebrows. 'Hey, maybe one of the skater-boys will give you *pointers* if you need them.'

Brendan cleared his throat. 'Um, Ivy, are you sure –'

But it was too late. Sophia was standing up. 'Fine,' she said, brushing off her jeans. 'I will.'

Ivy gasped. *Abort 'Tough Love', abort!* 'But . . .

you could hurt yourself!' *And you weren't supposed to call my bluff!*

'Don't be ridiculous.' Sophia stepped neatly out of reach and walked calmly over to the crowded skatepark. As skaters turned to stare, she set her board down and placed one foot on it. Then she pushed forward . . . and her vampire super-strength made the skateboard fly into the air in front of her, leaving her staggering so hard, she almost fell over.

I can't watch this! Ivy thought, hiding her face in her hands. But she couldn't help peeping through her fingers as the skateboard went soaring. The other skaters scrambled to get out of its way.

'Hey!' One of Finn's friends glared at her. 'We don't need a clown. This isn't a circus!'

The other guys all burst into laughter – all except Finn. He just looked away politely as Sophia hurried through the crowd, her shoulders hunched, to reclaim her skateboard from where it lay tipped on one side at the other end of the park.

Ivy cringed as Sophia stood back on the board. This time it didn't go flying – but it wobbled so badly, she teetered from side to side, forced to wave her arms wildly to keep her balance. Within five seconds, she had fallen right off.

'This is awful,' Brendan whispered to Ivy.

Ivy groaned in agreement as she glanced around at the crowd that was gathering – bunnies and goths all coming to watch and enjoy the 'comedy'. Her teeth ground together with frustration.

I can't just physically drag *her away. That would humiliate her even more!*

It took everything she had, though, to hold herself back as she watched Sophia fall again and again. The crowd snorted with laughter every time. Sophia hadn't wanted their old friends to see her embarrassing herself – but she was doing a good job of letting these new kids laugh at her expense.

Just give up, Ivy begged her friend silently.

At last, Sophia picked up her skateboard. Her face was flushed, but she held her chin high as she carried it by her side, walking away from the skatepark with as much dignity as she could muster.

Ivy let out a sigh of relief as she hurried to join her friend. 'You did the smart thing,' she whispered. She started to hold out her arms to give a comforting hug, but Sophia shook her head.

'Not in front of them,' she whispered back.

Ivy nodded and shoved her hands into her pockets. As Brendan scooped up Sophia's backpack, she sought for a way to cheer up her friend. 'You know,' she said, 'you could probably skateboard successfully if you just lost those shades.'

'No way!' Sophia's free hand went protectively

to her face. 'They're staying.'

Ivy shrugged, sighing. 'If you say so.'

Vampires had natural super-strength and super-speed . . . but, apparently, they did not always have super-common sense!

Brendan handed Sophia her backpack, and they started walking away from the skatepark, ignoring the laughter of the skaters behind them. As they passed a group of goths lounging nearby, Ivy saw that Amelia Thompson was looking from Finn to Sophia and back . . . and then gave Sophia a hard glare.

'Goths probably aren't allowed to skateboard either,' Ivy muttered, rolling her eyes. 'Or have any other kind of fun.' Which did make her wonder – what was Amelia doing in the park at all? *Shouldn't she be moping in a darkened room or something?*

Sophia only shrugged . . . but unfortunately, the movement made her backpack gape open and the gingham fabric spilled out.

Amelia's lips curled. She turned as if to speak to her friends, but her voice was pitched perfectly to reach Sophia and the others. 'Oh, yeah. Gingham is so *cute* . . . for a farmer. Don't you think?'

Her followers all laughed, like good little lackeys. Ivy's jaw clenched. 'That's it,' she said. 'I'm going to –'

Sophia grabbed her arm and pulled her forwards. 'Just forget it, Ivy.'

'Don't engage,' Brendan agreed in a whisper. 'It'll only cause more trouble.'

Reluctantly, Ivy gave in. She breathed a sigh of relief the moment they stepped out of the park. At least now, they wouldn't have anyone watching their every movement any more. Or would they? A curtain twitched across the street. Another twitched nearby. A moment later, a whole group of bunnies came flooding out of the first house, while goth underlings came hurrying from the park.

'Ivy! I'm having a party on Saturday. Do you want to come?'

'Hey, Ivy, we're having a barbecue next week. Will you be there?'

'Ivy, do you want to come to my house sometime? Just to hang out?'

Hang out? Ivy stared at the girl who'd made the suggestion. *I've never even seen her before. What would we even talk about?*

Sophia's voice quivered with laughter as she whispered into Ivy's ear, 'How does it feel to be Ms Popular?'

Ivy had to bite back a groan of horror. Sophia was right! Somehow, in this crazy town and school, she had actually become popular. *This was not supposed to happen!*

She looked at the crowd of waiting, expectant faces all around her and resolved to do something about this. She needed help to deal with her new circumstances.

Next time I talk to Olivia, she vowed, *I will ask her: how does* anyone *survive being popular?*

Chapter Six

'Aaaaand *cut*!'

Olivia's shoulders slumped with relief as the cameras stopped recording. She could barely breathe. *How did real Victorian women wear corsets every day without suffocating?*

But wearing corsets all the time still couldn't have been more annoying for Victorian girls than Olivia's afternoon had been for her – thirty-seven takes of walking into a room and gasping, followed by twenty-two takes of her looking out of a window 'wistfully'.

At this rate, I may graduate from college *before we finish this film!*

'And with that, we are wrapped tight and cosy for today!' Jacob Harker bellowed – even though calling an end to the day's filming should have been Tom the director's job. 'Out-race dawn to the set tomorrow, folks.'

I assume he just means 'bright and early', Olivia thought as she made her way off the set towards her trailer as quickly as she could. Unfortunately, that wasn't very quick. Her burgundy silk dress might have been drop-dead gorgeous, but between her fluffy bell-shaped skirt and tight ankle-length petticoat, walking was suddenly a *serious* challenge.

And tomorrow I have to somehow dance in this outfit! She let out a groan. *How is that supposed to happen?*

As she walked through the maze of production trucks and trailers parked outside the posh mansion where they had been filming, Olivia spotted Jackson standing with his back to her outside one of the trailers. He was dressed in his 'poor' Victorian costume, flipping through a script, and his shoulders were hunched.

Olivia frowned. Was he just concentrating hard? Or was he nervous? *That's so unlike him.* She hesitated, looking at his hunched shoulders. *Could he be nervous because of us?*

Their afternoon in London had been wonderful, but things had turned awkward again as soon as they'd started filming yesterday. *Then again . . .* Olivia sighed. They were playing people who were supposed to be in love with each other! For a real-life ex-couple, that was a tense situation to be in. How could they *not* feel awkward in this situation?

Maybe if she could lighten things up somehow . . .

All of a sudden, as Olivia stared at Jackson's back, she felt an overwhelming urge to sneak up behind him, cover his eyes and say, '*Guess who?*'

Don't be ridiculous! she told herself. *Why would*

anyone, in the history of anything, ever *think that was a good idea?*

She turned away, shaking her head, then stopped. Because really . . .

She'd seen it in so many movies that it was actually kind of traditional, wasn't it? Especially on a movie set! And even if it wasn't . . . *I have to do something to break this tension between us!*

Finally making a decision, she crept up behind him. Her big skirt rustled as she moved, but Jackson was studying his script too intensely to notice, even when she was less than a foot behind him. She stood up on tiptoe to reach out and cover his eyes . . .

Oh no! Her feet were tangled in her tight chemise. Olivia lurched forward, hopelessly off-balance . . . and landed right on Jackson's back, knocking him to the ground and landing right on top of him. She could feel his body wriggling beneath her and his grunts of protest, but there was nothing she could do to roll off him – not in this ridiculous dress. Loose script-pages fluttered everywhere.

Olivia closed her eyes in anguish. *Could that possibly have gone any worse?*

The answer was definitely *I don't think so.*

Her cheeks burned with embarrassment as she finally rolled off Jackson in her enormous hoop-skirt. She sat beside Jackson's fallen body, her cheeks still flushed and her breath coming in gasps because of the corset.

'I'm so sorry,' she wheezed. 'I didn't –'

She cut herself off with a gasp as Jackson turned to face her. *Oh no.*

She'd been wrong. It *could* have gone worse. It *had* gone worse. Much worse!

Because it wasn't Jackson she had tackled, after all. She'd taken a total *stranger* to the ground!

'I'm so sorry,' she repeated faintly. She felt

light-headed, and for once, it wasn't the corset that was to blame.

The stranger's hair was the same shade of blond as Jackson's and cut in the same hairstyle. He was the same height as Jackson, and he wore Jackson's costume . . . but he was definitely *not* Jackson.

'I-I-I . . .' Olivia stammered, scooting backwards. 'I'm so sorry, but you look *just* like . . .'

The stranger smiled ruefully. '. . . Jackson Caulfield?' he finished for her.

Olivia swallowed hard. 'Yes,' she admitted. 'How did you know?'

'Because I get that a lot.' The boy's smile turned into a grin. 'I'm Will, Jackson's body double.'

Olivia's eyes widened. 'Oh, of course! That explains it. But I didn't know we were getting body doubles!'

He nodded. 'You're Olivia Abbott, aren't you?'

'I am,' Olivia said. 'It's nice to meet you.' She started to reach out for a handshake – then cringed as she suddenly realised that Will was still lying spread-eagled on the ground, where she'd left him. 'I really am *so* sorry. I just lost my balance with this crazy dress!'

'No worries.' Will took her hand so they could help each other up. 'It was kind of fun to stop being Jackson's body double for a while, and be his *stunt* double!'

Olivia laughed with him as she smoothed down her skirt with her free hand. 'I promise not to make you perform any more surprise stunts!'

Will grinned, leaning a little closer. 'I don't know. This one was kind of fun.'

A flutter of curtain movement caught Olivia's eye. It was coming from a nearby trailer . . . *Jackson's* trailer. And Jackson stood at the window, scowling. *Oh no!*

She lunged backwards, pulling free of Will's

hand. *Jackson just saw me holding hands with another boy and laughing. What will he think?*

Then she saw the look on Will's face. He was staring down at her hand, which she had just yanked away from him with full force.

'Sorry,' he mumbled. 'I didn't mean to annoy you.'

'Oh, you didn't!' Olivia bit her lip, cringing at her own clumsiness. Will had been so nice about being knocked over in her mistaken joke. The last thing she wanted to do now was make him feel bad.

'I know I'm not one of the stars,' he said. 'If you felt like I was stepping out of line –'

'No, that's not it at all!' Olivia bit back a groan. *Why is this all so complicated?* She was all too aware of Jackson watching. Everything in her wanted to get away before he leaped to any false conclusions.

But she certainly didn't want Will to think she

found him . . . well, whatever it was he thought! And honestly, only a blind girl would think he was anything but attractive. In fact, being a good double for Jackson meant he was probably the second cutest boy on the whole planet!

His hair flopped forwards in just the right way, he had broad shoulders and a gorgeous spattering of freckles across his nose – plus eyelashes that any girl would die for. She opened her mouth to tell him that . . . then caught herself just in time.

Stop now! she ordered herself, in her best imagined Ivy-voice. *Don't create even more confusion!*

She gave another frustrated, side-long look at Jackson's trailer, and then rolled her eyes at herself. *This is ridiculous. Why should I be so embarrassed?*

She hadn't flirted with Will, she'd only been friendly. And even if she *had* been flirting, Jackson would have had no right to be angry. After all, they were not together.

And I can't let myself forget that, Olivia told herself. *It doesn't matter how many scenes we shoot together of a couple in love. It's just acting.*

So she hadn't done anything wrong . . . but that didn't make her feel any better as she said goodbye to Will and walked to her trailer. It felt as though she was surrounded by an invisible storm cloud of gloom – a storm that she'd brought on.

🦇　　　🦇　　　🦇

After what felt like a year later, Olivia was finally out of her costume and lying on the bed in her opulent, lushly carpeted trailer, wearing loose grey sweatpants and a pink-and-white Franklin Grove cheer-squad T-shirt. After her long day in a corset and Victorian hoop-skirt, though, she couldn't imagine wearing anything more comfortable. *If only all those journalists could see me now*, she thought. *I sure don't* look *like a movie star!*

When she'd first seen her trailer, she'd wondered why on earth it would include a bed as well as all the other luxuries, like the micro-wave and the flat-screen TV. Those might make some sense, but a bed? Surely she'd never sleep on the set!

Now, though, she just wanted to curl up in her comfy sweatpants and pretend that none of the last half-hour had happened. As she pulled the sheets over her head, she let out a sigh of relief.

Then she heard a familiar *ping!* coming from her laptop, which sat on the table by her elaborate kitchen unit. She knew that *ping*! It signalled an incoming message from the Lonely Echo messaging system on the Vorld Vide Veb, the vampire Internet . . . and there was only one person in the world who would contact her that way.

Ivy!

With a burst of renewed energy, Olivia threw off her covers and ran over to her laptop, waving at her twin. 'I am so happy to see you!'

she said. 'How's high school?'

Ivy looked out of the computer screen with big, anguished violet eyes. 'Horrible,' she announced, in an Eeyore-like Voice of Doom. 'I'm *popular*.'

'What?!' Olivia stared at her sister as she pulled out a chair by the table. Of all the bizarre things that had ever come out of Ivy's mouth, this had to be the most unexpected. 'Is that a joke?'

'I only wish it was.' Ivy buried her face in her hands. 'I need your help.'

Olivia sat down in front of the laptop, her own worries forgotten. 'Anything you need,' she said firmly. 'Just tell me all about it.'

As she watched, Ivy drew a deep breath. 'The goths,' Ivy announced, 'are the in-crowd. There are just *so many* of them! And . . .' Ivy's eyes looked wild. 'I really need to ask: how did *you* deal with being popular at school? Because I've only been dealing with it for three days, and I already want to nail my coffin shut so I don't have to face it any more!'

Olivia let out a snort. 'Me? "Popular"?' She shook her head as she leaned to grab a fresh strawberry-banana smoothie from her mini-fridge. 'Have you already forgotten? All of my friends were goths or sci-fi nerds. Remember?'

'Oh, yeah.' Ivy's shoulders slumped. 'Now that you're a big Hollywood star, I sometimes forget you weren't always that way.'

'Hmmph.' Olivia rolled her eyes and took a long sip of the sweet, cold smoothie. 'Speaking of my friends, though . . . how is Camilla?'

'Oh.' Ivy winced. 'I don't actually know. Sorry! She's going to Willowton High, and it's hard to get a word in when we're riding the bus with Charlotte. But I'll catch up with her, I promise!'

'Don't worry,' Olivia said, seeing her sister looking as gloomy as the black and dull-crimson hangings of her bedroom. 'How are the others doing?' Olivia asked, trying to change the subject.

Ivy let out a groan. 'I think Sophia's having some kind of breakdown!' Olivia's twin leaned forward, whispering: 'She's taken to wearing *gingham*.'

'*No way.*' Olivia almost dropped her smoothie.

'It's true.' Ivy shook her head. 'She's also become permanently attached to her shades and she's taken up skateboarding . . . or at least, she's tried.' Ivy looked pained. 'It hasn't gone very well so far.'

'But what's going on?' Olivia asked. 'Sophia's always been so fashion-conscious! I've never even seen her wear an *earring* that wasn't black.'

Ivy picked up a bat-figurine from her desk and scowled down at it. 'Well, she's changed now, big-time.'

Olivia stirred her smoothie with its straw, frowning. 'Could she just be trying really hard to fit in at the new school?'

'If that's the case, it isn't working.' Ivy grimaced. 'If anything, she's drawing *bad* attention to herself from our school's Queen Bee, Amelia. I don't think she can stand any goths acting un-gothlike.'

'Ouch.' Olivia winced in sympathy. 'I wish I could help.'

'I wish you could, too.' Ivy let out a sigh. 'I guess I was hoping you'd be able to help me with everything – my popularity problem and Sophia's weird behaviour.'

Olivia shrugged helplessly. 'If you think of anything I *can* do from thousands of miles away . . .'

'I don't know. Maybe just scream some sense into everybody, long-distance?' Ivy gave her a crooked grin. 'Still, it's really helped just talking to you about it. But I'd better go now. I've got some last minute homework to cram in. There's a *lot* more of that in high school!'

'I'll bet,' Olivia said, returning the smile. 'Good luck with it!'

After Ivy clicked off, Olivia sat for a long moment gazing sightlessly at the computer screen. Her smoothie was still mostly full, but she set it down on the table and tuned her ears to the buzz of activity outside her trailer. Movie-set activity – a world away from queen bees, popularity and homework . . .

Ivy's life was so different to Olivia's. It was *normal*. With this glamorous Hollywood contract, Olivia had signed away all her chances for normal education and even normal teenage drama. Maybe that should have been a relief, but it wasn't. As much as she loved the excitement of the movie set, part of her wished she was just hanging out in Franklin Grove with regular, normal vampires.

Ha! She couldn't help smiling at herself as she picked up the smoothie and took a long, cold sip.

Her life really had changed beyond recognition! Once upon a time, she would have thought that the whole idea of vampires was *totally* weird and scary. But now . . .

Her thoughts were cut off by a sudden shout outside her trailer. Choking on her mouthful of smoothie, she set down the cup and ran to her window.

'No, no, no!' A woman's voice roared through the air as Olivia lifted the curtain at her window. 'Try harder!'

Olivia almost didn't recognise Jackson with a scowl on his face, storming through the maze of production trucks and trailers. His hands were clenched into fists as he was followed by a short, squat, middle-aged woman. She shouted after him in an exaggerated "Cockney" voice.

'It's "a-*rand* the corner", not "a-*round* the corner" . . . You utter, utter *plonker*!'

Olivia's mouth dropped open. It was Jackson's

dialect coach, Ingrid . . . who seemed to be the meanest woman in the world!

Before she could think twice, she lunged for the door. *Someone* needed to stand up for Jackson and tell that woman that she'd gone over the edge! How could anyone think that treating an actor this way would get them to do their best work on set?

In her loose sweatpants and T-shirt, it was easy to move quickly. As soon as Olivia reached Ingrid, she opened her mouth to let loose – but Jackson gave her a light shake of the head, making the message clear: *Don't get in the middle of this.*

Olivia stared at him. Didn't he *want* to be defended?

Ingrid kept shouting: 'Apples and pears! A Weaver's Chair! The Top of Rome!'

Was she insulting him, or setting him really bizarre riddles? Olivia had no clue. But the cruel tone of Ingrid's voice was clear.

'Can't you keep any of them straight, with all the bread you're getting for this tosh? Use your loaf!'

I may not have any idea what she's saying, Olivia thought, crossing her arms, *but I know that I don't like her.*

Jackson didn't argue back, though. He only smiled tightly. 'I'll work on it, Ingrid,' he said. 'I promise. I *am* taking this seriously. It's just . . .' His gaze fell briefly on Olivia. '. . . I've got a lot on me mind right now. But I am focused.'

The accent was much better there, Olivia thought, aware of the strange fluttering in her chest, *when you're speaking from the heart.*

'Huh.' Ingrid snorted in obvious disbelief. 'We'll see about that tomorrow. *Early.* We'll go over your script together before shooting resumes – so that *you* don't sound like a total wally on-screen!'

Olivia gritted her teeth and waited for Ingrid to walk away before she walked over to Jackson. In a voice pitched too quietly for anyone else to hear, she asked, 'Are you OK?'

'Yah, I'm awight.' Jackson shrugged, keeping a nasal Cockney twang in his voice. 'I been yelled at afore, ye know? She's just been yakking on all afternoon about it. It's really narking me.'

'*Oh.*' Olivia's eyes widened. 'Is *that* why you looked so grumpy when I saw you in your trailer window just now?'

Grimacing, Jackson nodded. 'I shouldn'ta got the 'ump like what I did, but . . .' He dropped the Cockney accent. 'Wait a minute. Why did *you* think I was grumpy? What were you worried about?'

'Oh . . . nothing.' Olivia smiled, feeling a weight drop off her shoulders.

He hadn't been angry at her, or at Will. *I should have known better.* When had Jackson ever been unreasonable?

He was frowning now, though, as he looked down at her. 'Are you sure?' he said. 'You look so relieved –'

'I'm fine!' Olivia said. Hastily, she changed the subject. 'But how can you handle being yelled at so much?'

'Oh, well.' Jackson flashed the smile Olivia had seen on movie posters and in dozens of magazines. 'It's easier to take when you can barely understand what's being yelled!'

'I guess so.' Olivia wrinkled her nose. 'But still –'

'It's *normal* for the movie business.' Jackson shrugged. 'You get used to it after a while.'

'Really?' Olivia looked around the bustling maze of production trucks and trailers with fresh eyes. 'Yuck.' Instinctively, she took another step closer to Jackson. 'I mean, I've read about movie set drama in magazines, but . . . it's different to see and hear it for myself.' She shook her head. 'And I just don't understand how anyone can accept that kind of meanness as *normal*. And what kind of person would *be* that mean in the first place?'

'Honestly, there aren't that many bad folks,' Jackson said. 'It's just that everybody's under so much pressure.' He leaned closer to her, smiling reassuringly. 'Don't worry. The more you work, the more used to it you'll get. You'll develop a tough shell to protect yourself, just like the rest of us do.'

Olivia couldn't stop her expression from twisting into uncertainty. *But do I really want that? Do I really want to jump into a world where people are so crazy with stress and worry that they are* this *mean to each other?*

She looked down to hide her expression from Jackson . . . but she was too late. He must have sensed her feelings. She saw his hand start to reach for hers. Time seemed to slow down around them as she held her breath, waiting for their fingers to touch. It was as if they were inside an invisible bubble, separating them from all the bustle and noise of film production. Just her and Jackson, together . . .

Then his hand paused and fell away. Olivia felt a stab of pain in her chest as the bubble popped.

Maybe being on set together wasn't going to fix everything the way that she had hoped. Maybe their lives weren't compatible after all. No matter how much she cared about Jackson, could she be sure that taking on the whole Hollywood lifestyle was the right choice for *her*?

Olivia wanted to shout at the sky. *This is so unfair!*

Jackson took a step back and drew an audible, deep breath. When he spoke again, his Cockney twang was back in full swing. 'Look, I'm sorry, but I gotter dive – 'Arker said 'e'd need me on set now.'

Now that she did finally look up, Olivia could see Jackson staring at his watch. Was that why he'd let go of her hand – because he was running late? He started to turn away, then hesitated. 'What're ye doin' on Satahdee?'

'"Satahdee?"' Olivia repeated blankly. 'Oh, *Saturday*! Nothing, I don't think. I mean, I don't have any plans. We have the weekend off, don't we?'

'That's right,' Jackson said, 'and I was finkin' . . . d'ye wanna take a nanny-ride along the Thames shake?'

'A *what*?' Olivia stared at him.

He grinned. '"Nanny-goat,"' he said. 'That means *boat,* and "shake" means *river*. I'm asking you for a boat-ride along the Thames.'

'Oh. I get it . . . I think,' Olivia said. Was a boat-ride with Jackson a good idea or a really, really bad one? She felt so numb, she couldn't even tell. 'That sounds good,' she said weakly.

'Cushty,' Jackson said. Olivia assumed that meant, *Good*. He swung off, striding quickly through the cluster of trailers and trucks. Just before he disappeared from sight, Olivia heard him greeting Harker. 'Awight, Guv'ner?'

Ingrid's voice rapped out furiously from somewhere nearby: 'That's "Guv-*nah*"!'

Wincing, Olivia turned away. It was almost time for her parents to collect her from her trailer . . . and she still hadn't come to any conclusions about Jackson, or about herself.

What ever happened to figuring things out?

~~   ~~   ~~

The next day, Ivy sat with Brendan at the very back of the school bus, as usual, but Sophia was nowhere to be seen.

'What do you think?' Ivy whispered to her boyfriend, as the big banana-coloured bus rolled down the street towards the school. 'Is she sick? Or is she just having a last-minute gingham emergency?'

'Ugh.' Brendan grimaced. 'Maybe she's just

got really, really into the whole subterfuge thing? Trying to be un-vamp-y, like our parents want?'

'No way.' Ivy kept her voice too low for the students in front of them to hear. 'Trust me, she's not doing this for her parents. She'd never do anything that stupid for them. She has to be doing it for a boy.'

'Really? *Sophia*?' Brendan stretched out his legs under the seat in front of him, looking sceptical. 'I don't know. She's always been smarter than that.'

'I talked it all over with Lillian last night,' Ivy told him. 'She says it's not uncommon for girls to do the stupidest things to impress boys.'

A lock of dark hair flopped over Brendan's eyes as he shook his head, letting out a half-laugh. 'I've never seen *you* do anything like that.'

'No?' Ivy nudged him playfully. 'Remember when we were in elementary school, and I was "really, *really* into" Ninja Warrior 7?'

'You were?' Brendan frowned.

'Oh that's right, I forgot,' Ivy laughed. 'You ignored me all through our childhood.'

'I did not,' Brendan protested.

Ivy gave his hand a squeeze. 'The point is, I *mastered* that game, just because you once wore a Ninja Warrior 7 T-shirt!'

'Are you kidding?' Brendan stared at her for a long moment. Then he started to laugh, even as he wrapped one arm around her shoulder to hug her close. 'I didn't even like the game! The shirt was a Christmas present from my mom . . . and I only ever wore it *once.*'

'Argh!' Ivy groaned and buried her face in his shoulder. 'I wasted a whole summer on that game, just in case you ever invited me over to your house to play it. I was going to impress you with my mad Ninja skills!'

'Aww.' Brendan tipped up her chin and kissed her. 'Ivy Vega, you are a tremendous dork.'

'Whatever!' Ivy whispered back. As the bus jerked to a stop in front of the school grounds, she gave him a mischievous grin. 'You just love me for my Ninja powers, and you know it!'

Still laughing, she jumped up to follow the students in front of her off the bus, while Brendan playfully hung on to her backpack. She stepped off the bus – and then leaped back, gasping and almost knocking Brendan over, as a flash of black and white gingham swooped past.

Was it a bird, was it a plane . . .?

Oh no. It's worse!

Ivy cringed as she recognised Sophia, her skateboard swerving dangerously towards a collection of stone benches on the school grounds.

'Look out!' Brendan yelled.

Ivy could only watch, speechless with horror, as Sophia's skateboard took another violent swerve. Sophia's sunglasses fell from her face, just in time for her to see the bench rising up in front of her. With a super-agile vampire leap, she hopped straight over the bench as her skateboard whizzed beneath it.

Ivy counted it as an absolute miracle when Sophia landed back on the board on the other side of the bench and turned to wobble back over to her friends.

Ivy caught her up halfway. 'Do you have any idea how close you came to being rushed to the nearest emergency room?' She pointed at the skateboard under Sophia's feet. 'Stop riding that thing!'

But Sophia obviously wasn't listening. Instead, she was gazing directly over Ivy's shoulder at something that made her lips curve into a dreamy smile. Using the skateboard to shoot away from Ivy, she scooped up her sunglasses from the ground and shoved them back on her nose.

'And that's another thing!' Ivy yelled after her

friend. 'Stop wearing those things! They're not good for your health!'

Brendan came up beside her, shaking his head. 'You do realise she isn't paying any attention to you.'

'I know,' Ivy said glumly, as they watched Sophia aim her skateboard at the group of skater-boys and girls gathered near the front of the school building. She was clearly intent on joining them . . . but in her rush, she seemed to have forgotten how to put on the brakes. She tried to stop, but it was too late. Her arms windmilled through the air.

As Ivy let out a moan of sympathetic horror, Sophia skated her board right over Finn's feet.

'Please tell me I imagined that,' Ivy breathed.

'I wish you had,' Brendan whispered back.

Together, they started running, even as the group of blonde skater-girls near Finn all started screaming at once.

Every time Ivy had ever seen Finn, he had been wearing pristine white tennis shoes. They'd been so perfectly white, Ivy could have written an essay on them. Now, though, Ivy could see dirty black wheel marks running over the top of them.

She cringed at the sight. *It's like a sign saying, 'Sophia was here!'*

Sophia's face was bright red, and her words were tumbling over each other as the skater-girls all glared at her from behind Finn, whispering to each other.

'I am just so, so sorry!' Sophia gasped. 'I never meant – I would never, ever, ever, on purpose . . .'

Ivy started forwards to save her out-of-control friend, but Brendan pulled her gently to one side. 'Shh,' he whispered. 'Look again.' He nodded at Finn, and Ivy followed his gaze.

Finn didn't look angry. He didn't even look annoyed.

'Hey, don't worry,' he said, smiling at Sophia,

his eyes twinkling. 'It's fine. Totally! I was getting desperate for ways to scuff up these new shoes anyway. You've done me a triumphant favour.'

'Really?' Sophia bit her lip.

Finn clamped a reassuring hand on her shoulder. His blond hair glinted in the sunlight, and his smile was dazzling. 'Absolutely. Don't worry about it, OK?'

'OK,' Sophia breathed. Her eyes were shining. As Ivy watched, Sophia's gaze drifted over to his fingers, still resting on her shoulder. Her lips trembled.

'See you around!' Finn gave her shoulder one more squeeze, then wandered off with his gang of friends.

Sophia turned slowly, as if in a daze, to Ivy and Brendan. 'He . . . he touched my shoulder!' she whispered.

Ivy rolled her eyes. 'We saw.'

The school bell rang, harsh and jangling, but it

wasn't enough to jolt Sophia back into common sense. Her eyes were glazed with delight even as Ivy turned her around and shoved her gently towards the school building.

We are going to have to have a real talk soon, Ivy thought grimly. *Away from all skateboards and sunglasses!*

There might not be time to fix Sophia now, but at least Ivy had finally solved one mystery. Lillian had been right, as usual. Sophia *was* being driven by a huge crush . . . on Skater Finn!

Chapter Seven

Snap out of it! Olivia told herself.

She was on the deck of a yacht, cruising directly past Hampton Court Palace. It should have been one of the coolest moments of her entire life, but all she could think about was the boy next to her. *Jackson*.

What was he really thinking as he leaned over her shoulder, pointing out London landmarks? What did he *want* from her, and for their relationship? And what did *Olivia* want for herself?

Hampton Court Palace was impressive. Apparently, Henry VIII had once lived there. Admittedly, Olivia knew less about English history than she did about quantum physics, but Jackson was full of fun facts. The palace sprawled along the riverbank like something out of a fairy tale, but Olivia was very much *not* enchanted by it.

Then Ivy's brisk voice in her head answered her question: *Stop being silly and enjoy this experience!*

Right. Olivia focused on the lapping waves, and the long-necked swans that floated past the yacht. *Be in the moment*, she told herself.

And what a moment it was! The yacht had been privately rented by Jackson just so that the cast and crew could have a special treat at the end of Week One. *That's so Jackson, thinking of everyone!* All around them, people were milling about, carrying crystal flutes filled with pomegranate juice or elderflower spritzers, and there were whole tables covered in sparkling white linen tablecloths and platters of food.

Olivia loved seeing so much history floating

past her . . . and better yet, she didn't even have to wear a corset to enjoy it! Instead, she was wearing her favourite light pink, knee-length sundress. She had *never* appreciated loose-fitting contemporary clothing so much until she had spent a week dressing like a Victorian!

Smiling, Olivia took a deep breath just to prove that she could. *Thank goodness I live in the twenty-first century, and not the nineteenth! Breathing comfortably is definitely underrated.*

She couldn't wait to switch to 1950s style, when they got back to the States for their next block of shooting. *After corsets, poodle skirts sound like heaven!*

Now she looked around, hearing the hum of voices behind her. Olivia had spent the first part of the cruise mingling with the rest of the cast, while her parents hung out with the other actors' parents and guardians below deck. After half an hour, though, Jackson had asked Olivia if she wanted to walk with him along the deck, *alone* . . .

''Ave a butcher's at that!' he said now, pointing over her shoulder. 'Can ya believe all this 'istree, right in front of us!'

Olivia sighed, even as she smiled politely. It was hard to be thrilled by the *'istree* of anything!

She knew it was important for him to practise and stay in character. Better yet, she could see that it was paying off in his performance. Yesterday had been the best day of filming so far. Jackson had had to do a monologue twice, once in the posh voice and once in the Cockney, and even terrifying Ingrid, the Vocal Coach of Doom, had actually agreed that it was good.

It's not that I don't admire Jackson's commitment, Olivia thought glumly. *But it's hard to feel romantic when he sounds like a stranger.*

The sound of a throat being cleared behind her made her turn – and her momentary annoyance evaporated as she saw a waiter approaching with a platter of delicious-looking appetisers.

'Oh good!' Jackson stepped forward, smiling. 'I'm Dean Martin!'

The waiter rolled his eyes. 'No, you're *Hank Marvin*,' he said, in a *real* London accent.

'Are you sure?' Jackson frowned, looking suddenly less confident. 'I really thought I was Dean Martin.'

The waiter shook his head. 'No, you're *definitely* Hank Marvin.'

Are you both crazy? Olivia wanted to scream. *He's Jackson Caulfield!*

Then she bit back a groan as she realised what was going on. *Why can't anything just make sense?*

Ever since she'd arrived in London, it had felt like *everything* was in a code she couldn't read . . . from the language that everybody spoke to the feelings that Jackson might or might *not* have for her.

Still, she was pretty sure she could work out

this particular puzzle. *Hank Marvin* rhymed with . . . *starving!* Jackson must have meant he was hungry. And she was, too!

The waiter offered the platter to her. 'Miss?'

'Thank you.' *I can do this!* Olivia braced herself to make the attempt. 'I'm so . . . Sally . . . Tungry?'

For a moment, the waiter stared at her blankly. Then he burst out laughing.

Sighing, Olivia took a still-steaming spring roll and watched as he walked away, chuckling so much he almost dropped his platter.

'So, it's not something you can just make up on the spot?' she asked Jackson.

'Well . . .' He smiled sympathetically. 'Maybe if –'

But before he could finish, the yacht lurched to a stop. The sudden movement threw Olivia forward . . . straight into Jackson's arms.

Her spring roll fell to the deck as he caught her. His breath was warm against her hair. She thought she could feel his heartbeat racing – but that might have been her own.

Then the captain's voice blared over the intercom:

'Sorry about that, ladies and gentlemen. There's a slight mechanical difficulty down here, but the crew are working on it now. We should be on the move again shortly. In the meantime, everyone, just get comfy and enjoy the view.'

Olivia couldn't help it. She started laughing as Jackson helped her upright.

He didn't let go of her hands even after she was standing safely on the deck. 'What is it?' He looked down at her, his eyebrows raised. 'Why are you laughing?'

Olivia shook her head, smiling ruefully and wondering if there could possibly be a more perfect metaphor for their whole relationship than a stalled ship? *Surrounded by a wonderful view but going nowhere . . .*

'Nothing,' she said. 'Never mind.'

'Hey, hey, hey, *Eternal Sunset* cast and crew!' Mr Harker's voice suddenly boomed out of a megaphone, only ten feet behind Olivia.

She jumped, then pulled her hands free to clap them over her ears as she spun around. The vampire studio boss was grinning mischievously as he looked straight at her and Jackson.

'Since this yacht of ours isn't moving, we're going to have to create our *own* movement. And you guys know what that means . . .'

Do we? Olivia stared warily at Jackson, who closed his eyes and groaned, 'Oh no . . .'

Harker stepped back and gestured grandly at the big speakers set along the deck. A moment later, 1950s pop music blasted out from the speakers.

Silently, Olivia echoed Jackson's groan.

Just what this awkward afternoon needs – dancing!

🦇　　　🦇　　　🦇

Argh. Ivy groaned silently as she tipped her head against the window beside her seat on the bus as it stopped at yet another red light. *I'm on a bus going nowhere!*

She was very eager to get to the Lincoln Vale Mall – and was seriously worried about what she might find when she got there. She had gone to Sophia's house that afternoon to have a serious talk with her friend. Unfortunately, she'd been too late – and as soon as Sophia's mom had told her where her friend had gone, Ivy had been filled with panic.

If Sophia actually wanted to go shopping, Ivy had reasoned, *she would have gone to the Franklin Grove Mall.*

Was she hoping to run into Finn the skater-boy? Wasn't that what some people called 'stalking'?

Ivy had to stop her before she went too far.

Finally, the bus lurched back into movement.

When it pulled up in front of the Lincoln Grove Mall, Ivy jumped off with a moan of impatience. She hurtled through the front doors with only one goal. *Mission: Rescue Sophia – From Herself!*

But as she hurried down the long galleries of the mall, her eyes widened. As malls went, it was actually the coolest one she'd ever seen. One side was dominated by goth and alternative clothing outlets, the other with accessories stores. Pall Bearers CDs filled the display cases of the music stores. And right up there, in front of her . . .

Oh my darkness. Ivy's feet slowed to a stop as she stared at the mall's comic-book store, the frontage rising up and up over the central fountain. She had to tip her head all the way back to see the very top floor with its glass-fronted display. *That store is bigger than my whole house!*

She had to force her mouth shut before she could start moving again. *No time to stop!* she told herself firmly.

Still, she slid longing glances back at it as she walked away. *I will definitely bring Brendan here another time . . . when I'm not looking for my crazy best friend!*

Ivy turned a corner to find a bunch of middle-schoolers soaring down the polished gallery floor right towards her on their skateboards. She leapt aside just in time to avoid a messy crash.

One of the younger skateboarders craned his neck backwards as he skated past. 'Are you OK?'

Ivy sighed. 'I'm fine.'

The truth was, she could have leapt all the way across the gallery if she'd wanted to. Instead, she'd forced herself to use only half her strength and landed just far enough away for safety. She couldn't break the First Law of the Night by letting outsiders see her vampire super-strength at work.

But up ahead of her, she saw a vampire who didn't seem to remember anything about the

Laws of the Night – or who she really was – any more. Sophia – who looked like she had been caught in explosion at a gingham factory – stood in the middle of a line of skater-girls that snaked down the long gallery. *What are they in line for?*

Scowling, Ivy marched right up to her friend and tapped her on the shoulder.

Sophia gasped, her arms flying up to cover her gingham shirt.

Ivy rolled her eyes. 'Your arms are in the *sleeves* of your shirt, Sophia. You can't hide gingham by covering it up with gingham sleeves!'

Sophia looked at the floor. 'What are you even doing here?'

'Your mom told me where I could find you.' Ivy crossed her arms. 'But she didn't tell me *why* you'd come here in the first place.'

Sophia shrugged, lifting her chin defiantly. 'There's a special offer.'

'On what?'

Her friend didn't answer, so Ivy leaned out from the line of girls, craning her neck to see. The line ended in a hair salon, and the poster in front showed . . .

Ivy's mouth dropped open. 'You wouldn't!'

A short-haired, blonde girl smiled out from the poster. Her hairstyle was the same as worn by everyone in the flock of skater-girls from the park the other day – the ones who'd applauded Finn's 'bodacious cabs' as if their lives depended on it.

Half-Price Cut-and-Dye Today! read the banner at the bottom of the poster.

Ivy turned to stare at her friend. 'You cannot be serious.'

'Why not?' Sophia asked. She crossed her arms stubbornly. 'Are you turning into Amelia now, Ivy? Telling other goths what to wear?'

Ivy gasped. 'I am *not* like Amelia!'

'No?' From behind her sunglasses, Sophia

raised an accusatory eyebrow.

Taking a deep breath, Ivy forced herself to imagine her friend with short, blonde, pixie-style hair. But her brain simply refused to form the image.

'Look,' Ivy said. She fought to keep her voice soft and reasonable. 'At the risk of sounding like Charlotte Brown, have you actually stopped to think how this is going to *look*?'

Sophia's chin jutted out. 'I'll pull it off.'

Where was the vamp-fashionista Ivy had known her whole life? Taking a deep breath, she stepped closer. 'What will your parents say when you get home and reveal this new-look? They'll totally freak out.'

Sophia's jaw clenched, but she didn't back down. 'It'll be worth it.'

Ivy shook her head. Lowering her voice to a whisper, she hissed: 'You can't say that Finn is worth this much trouble and effort. You've known him for *one week*, and the most you've talked to him is when you fell down in front of him.'

'Finn has nothing to do with it,' Sophia hissed back. 'I just want to try a new look for our new school. That's all!'

Ivy sighed. *Yeah, right.* If her friend wasn't ready to admit to her crush, then Ivy wasn't about to humiliate her by pressing the point.

But as the line shuffled forwards, the entrance to the hair salon grew ominously close, like a whirlpool sucking in helpless sailors.

If I don't think of something fast, Ivy thought, *my best friend is going to make a horrible mistake. We don't have much time!*

🦇   🦇   🦇

We don't have much time! Olivia had to bite back an Ivy-like growl of frustration, even as her dance partner dipped her in a romantic twirl. She had never endured such an awful dance. It wasn't her partner's fault – Will, Jackson's body double, was

171

a fabulous dancer. But she'd been trying to get back to Jackson, without any success, ever since Mr Harker had first started blaring 50s music on the yacht.

For some reason, Jackson seemed to be exempt to Mr Harker's rule that everybody 'get down'. Instead, he sat typing on his tablet device, as if the rest of the cast and crew weren't spinning on the deck-turned-dance floor right in front of him.

Every time a new song ended, Olivia had made a move to cross the deck towards him. But – *every time* – she'd found another cast member walking into her path with a big smile and a hand held out to sweep her into the next dance. It was so smoothly done, she wondered if the whole thing had been choreographed!

As the latest song finished, she smiled and pulled away from Will as quickly as she could without being rude. She could feel Jackson's presence at the edge of the deck, like a magnet pulling her towards him. *Finally!* She started towards him . . .

. . . and Mr Harker beckoned her over. 'Olivia!'

Argh! As another track kicked in, Olivia forced herself not to let the annoyance show on her face. She couldn't offend the studio boss . . . even if she was ready to scream at yet another interruption!

'Yes?' she said politely. 'Did you want to dance?'

'Ha!' Mr Harker grinned. 'Don't sweat it.' He glanced meaningfully at where Jackson sat on the edge of the deck, still typing on his tablet device. 'I know exactly what busy bees are buzzing through your brain.'

'Then why are you *getting in my way*?' The words burst out of Olivia's mouth before she could stop them. Horrified at her own loss of control, she clapped her hand over her mouth . . . but it was too late to take the words back. *Way to tell him everything!*

Harker smiled and leaned closer to whisper in her ear. 'It's a basic rule of storytelling, kiddo – the longer the audience is made to wait, the better it feels when the characters finally get what they want.' As he straightened, he gave her an approving nod. 'But you're *not* the audience. Go get him!'

'Thank you!' Olivia breathed a sigh of relief as the studio boss made way for her with a dramatic, sweeping gesture.

Smoothing down her skirt, she started towards Jackson. *At last!* He was so focused on his tablet, he didn't see her approaching.

Olivia pasted a confident smile on her face. *I will make this happen. I will –*

'Aaah!' She let out a cry as the ground moved beneath her feet, throwing her forwards. The yacht had lurched back into motion again at just the wrong time!

She landed straight on top of Jackson,

knocking the tablet from his hand. As it crashed to the ground, she cringed. *Smooth move, Olivia!*

'Sorry!' She scrambled off him and reached for the tablet.

'No!' Jackson lunged forwards, almost knocking her aside. 'Don't!'

He grabbed the tablet from the deck and Olivia tried not to feel hurt. 'I wouldn't have dropped it,' she told him. 'I'm not *that* clumsy.'

'That's not what I . . .' Jackson inspected it hastily, then clicked the power off and hid it behind his back

Olivia blinked. *What is he trying to hide?*

He collected himself, taking a deep breath and flashing his megawatt smile. 'Anyway,' he said, and gestured down the deck in front of them with his free hand. 'Now that we're moving again, do you want to have a last look at the view?'

Are we already that close to the end of the trip? Olivia fought down panic as she followed him around the weather deck. Up ahead, she could see the dock that signalled the end of their boat ride, coming closer and closer with every moment. Jackson pointed out landmarks, talked charmingly about the weather and the film . . . but he didn't say a word – in *any* accent – about *them*.

Am I the only one being driven mad by this? Olivia wondered, forcing herself to smile and keep up her side of their conversation. All she could see, though, was the dock ahead of them. *Look at it*, she thought grimly, *all beautiful and opulent*. She had never before wanted anything so wonderful-looking to drift further and further *away* instead of closer!

Jackson was frowning at her. 'So you think it's a bad idea, then?'

'Huh?' Olivia snapped back out of her thoughts. *Uh-oh*. Jackson must have seen the look on her face, and thought it had been in response to something he'd said. But what *had* he been saying? She'd been so distracted she'd zoned out!

'Um . . . I'm not sure,' she hedged. 'What do *you* think?'

'Well, he seems OK to me,' Jackson said slowly. 'But I guess what I really wondered was, what *you* thought of him.'

Olivia's mind was blank. *Who are we talking about?*

Then she followed Jackson's gaze to where Will, his body double, stood at the other end of the deck, watching them.

'Oh, *Will!*' Olivia almost laughed with relief as she found her way back into the conversation. 'What do *I* think of him? Well . . .'

She remembered knocking him over in her hoop-skirt, when she'd thought that he was Jackson. Her face burned with renewed embarrassment.

A crease appeared in Jackson's brow. 'Why are you blushing?'

'Oh . . . no reason,' Olivia mumbled. 'Really. It's not worth explaining.'

'No?' Jackson's frown deepened. 'I'd really like to hear it, though.'

Silence pulsed between them as the dock grew closer and closer. *I can't tell him what happened,* Olivia thought. *It's too embarrassing!* But she had to say something to break the odd tension that was growing between them at that moment.

'Um, he's very convincing,' she said, 'as a body double, but . . .'

'But . . .?' Jackson asked.

'Well, he's nowhere near as kind and thoughtful as you are,' Olivia blurted. 'Who *could* be?'

Jackson let out a half-laugh, stepping back. 'You don't have to say that. Seriously –'

'I mean it!' She frowned at him, putting her hands on her hips. 'Honestly, who else would hire a boat for the entire crew?'

'Olivia . . .' Jackson shook his head, flushing.

'You know I like to do nice things for people.'

Olivia stepped forwards, closing the distance between them. 'I know, but even so . . . it's pretty awesome . . .'

Her words dried up as embarrassment hit her. *Am I really lecturing Jackson about himself?* 'I'm sorry,' she mumbled. She felt her face flush again. 'I've been talking too much, haven't I?'

'No,' Jackson said gently. He grinned, and this time it wasn't the smile from the posters and magazine covers. It was a smile Olivia knew from their time as a couple.

A personal smile, just for her.

He took her hand, looking straight into her eyes. 'Everything you say is absolutely perfect,' he said. 'In fact –'

Bump!

The yacht had hit the dock with a thud. Jackson's mouth snapped shut as he looked around nervously.

Suddenly, there were people streaming towards them from every direction, talking and laughing and eager to disembark.

Jackson let go of her hand. 'I guess it's time to go,' he said.

Olivia nodded. But as she looked at her ex-boyfriend-now-something-else, she felt an ache burn deep in her chest. 'It was a wonderful afternoon,' she said softly.

It was true.

But why was she now feeling anything but wonderful?

Chapter Eight

Ivy's stomach felt tight with dread as the line of skater-girls shuffled forwards, bringing the black leather hairdresser's chair closer and closer. *Sophia's really going to go through with this!*

They were fourth in line now, and the team of hairdressers was working fast – *too* fast! Ivy watched the latest identical blonde skater-girl emerge from the salon, beaming and stroking her identikit haircut. *It's like watching a parade of clones! Can't Sophia see that?*

The big, black chair looked ready to swallow up the next unique, individual girl and spit her out as yet another copy of *SkaterGirl 2.0*. If Ivy didn't think fast, the same thing was about to happen to her best friend.

If only Olivia was here! Ivy's twin would never have pressed the point so hard. She'd have been able to explain gently to Sophia just why this was such a terrible idea.

I don't have those skills! Ivy thought glumly.

How many more times could she simply repeat, 'It's not a good look for you'? Because, so far, that tactic was *not* working and she felt mean even saying it. *Telling people how they should look is* so not *'me'*.

'Next!' the top hairdresser announced.

Yet another skater girl jumped off the black chair, her hair magically transformed into exactly the same colour and cut as every other girl's before her.

Sophia beamed as she moved forwards in the line. Ivy's heart rate sped up. *I wonder just how much trouble I would get into for setting off this mall's fire alarm?*

'Oh, would you please stop scowling?' Sophia demanded, shaking her head at Ivy. 'What if this style is the "new me"?'

'It can't be!' Frantically, Ivy waved from the latest skater-girl to Sophia. 'They all look exactly the same. Just think about that.'

'No, *you* think about it.' Sophia slid her sunglasses down her nose and glared at Ivy. 'You seem to want me to look just the same as every other goth. How is that any different? Are you, of all people, seriously going to force another person to look a certain way? Just because it's the way *you* look? Because, if you are, then . . . there's really no difference between you and Amelia Thompson.'

Ivy stared at her friend, her jaw slack.

Sophia nudged her sunglasses back into place. Smiling serenely, she followed the line as it shuffled forwards yet again as one more skater clone strode proudly out of the salon. Numbly,

Ivy turned and followed after.

I can't stay and watch, she thought.

But Sophia was right: this decision was hers to make.

High school is pretty challenging, Ivy thought miserably. Her best friend was making a drastic mistake, all the social rules had been turned upside-down . . .

Things had seemed so much less serious back in eighth grade!

🦇   🦇   🦇

The next morning, Ivy couldn't stop clicking *refresh* on her emails in between checking her phone. Still no messages from Sophia. *Is she giving me the cold shoulder?*

Ivy didn't even know if they'd had a proper falling-out! *It didn't feel like it . . . but maybe that's only by middle school rules. Maybe by high school rules, I really offended her.*

As Ivy checked her phone one more time, she finally asked herself the real question she'd been dreading: *Are we even friends any more?*

'Why so glum?'

Ivy gave a start as Olivia's beaming face suddenly filled the computer screen, courtesy of the Lonely Echo messaging system.

'I have never been so glad to see you!' Ivy felt tears burn at the back of her eyes. 'I really need help.'

Olivia's smile turned into a concerned frown. 'Of course,' she said. 'What's wrong?'

'It's Sophia.' Ivy spilled out the whole story of their friend's transformation, ending with the madness at the mall. As she explained, she watched Olivia's face go pale with horror.

'A blonde pixie-cut?' Olivia gasped. 'That's crazy!'

'That's what I said!' Ivy swallowed hard. 'But

she just thought I was trying to force her into being a Goth Clone. Like I wasn't respecting her individuality.'

'It has nothing to do with individuality,' Olivia said. 'Sophia just doesn't have the colouring for blonde hair. It would look completely unnatural on her. It would make her look sallow! And, with the shape of her face, a pixie-cut is the least flattering style I can imagine. And she looks awesome just as she is!'

'I *knew* you'd find the right words to explain it.' Ivy smiled wearily. 'I could have used you yesterday.'

'But I wasn't there.' Olivia bit her lip, looking away. 'I'm so sorry . . .'

'Don't be.' Ivy shrugged, looking down at her silent phone. 'It's *my* fault, for not being able to talk her out of it.'

Her twin sighed. 'From what you've said, I'm not sure *anyone* could have talked Sophia out of it, if she was really determined to impress this "Finn" boy. She's never had a major crush before, has she?'

'No,' Ivy said.

Olivia shrugged. 'Then this one must be hitting her extra-hard.'

'It's probably just a phase, though, right?' Ivy twirled the bat-ring on her finger nervously. 'I mean, most girls grow out of their first crushes pretty quickly, don't they?'

'Um . . .' Olivia looked meaningfully at the ring Ivy was twirling on her finger . . . a ring given to her by Brendan. 'Maybe *some* girls do,' she said.

Ivy followed Olivia's gaze to her finger and groaned, letting go of her ring as if it had burned her. 'You're right! My first crush was Brendan, all those years ago, and yours –'

'– was Jackson,' Olivia finished softly.

They looked at each other, wide-eyed. Then they both began to laugh.

'I guess we're hardly ones to talk,' said Olivia

Ivy leaned back in her chair, idly picking up a glass of Strawberry HemoGlobules and taking a long sip through her ruby-red straw. 'So,' she said, 'speaking of Jackson, how's everything going on-set?'

'Honestly?' Olivia let out a groan and tipped her head into her hands.

Ivy winced and set down her drink. 'That bad?'

'The work is great,' Olivia said, her voice muffled by her hands. 'The work is fabulous. But *Jackson* . . .'

Ivy's shoulders stiffened. She could feel the beginnings of a death-squint. 'What has he done?'

'Nothing,' Olivia said, her eyes filled with frustration. 'That's the problem. He took me on a boat ride yesterday down the Thames.'

Sitting back, Ivy raised her eyebrows. 'Sounds . . . romantic?'

'Well, I thought so,' Olivia said. 'I thought he

was going to *say* something romantic, or make some kind of declaration. But it turned out . . . he just wanted to go on the boat ride!'

Ivy grimaced sympathetically. 'So what now?'

'Now we're in London for just one more day before production goes on a break,' Olivia said. 'Then he'll be going back to Hollywood, and I'll be coming home. And *nothing* will have changed!'

Ivy frowned. 'You're not done with shooting yet, are you?'

'But when we start shooting again, we'll be doing scenes without each other!' Olivia slumped. 'I know you think film sets must be great, but they're a lot less fun without the boy you love.'

Ivy fought to keep her mouth from dropping open. In her lap, her phone began to ring for the first time in twenty-four hours. She'd been waiting all day to hear that sound . . . but now she ignored it.

Did Olivia even realise she'd just finally let slip her true feelings?

'Olivia . . .' she began, as her phone vibrated beside her. It shook harder and harder with every ring. By the fourth ring, it was vibrating so hard, it was practically doing a jig on the table.

'Don't worry,' Olivia said. Sighing, she straightened. 'I can hear your phone ringing, and I have to get to make-up now, anyway. We'll talk later.'

'Are you sure?' Ivy asked. 'If you need to talk now –'

But her twin just gave a sad wave before flicking off her webcam.

Ivy let out a groan of frustration. *Talk about awful timing!*

'Yes?' she snapped into her cell phone. 'What is it?'

'Ivy . . .' It was Brendan, and he didn't sound happy either. 'You need to get over here. Fast.'

'Where are you?' Ivy was already starting up from her computer desk and hunting for her boots in her messy bedroom. 'What's wrong?'

Out of the corner of her eye, she spotted the tip of one black boot peeking out from under her bed. She dived for it just as Brendan answered:

'I'm in the Lincoln Vale skatepark.'

Ivy groaned. With her head still halfway under her bed, she asked, 'Is Sophia there?'

'For now.' Brendan's tone was grim. 'But, pretty soon, she'll be in the emergency room if she keeps falling off that skateboard.'

Ivy pulled herself up to sit on the cluttered floor by the bed, leaving the boot lying abandoned nearby. 'I don't know if it's a good idea for me to show up there,' she mumbled, drawing her knees up to her chest. 'I don't think Sophia wants to see me right now. We're . . . we're not exactly best friends at the moment.'

'Stop talking nonsense.' Brendan's words

rapped out, making Ivy gasp.

She'd never heard him sound so tough on her before!

He barely paused for breath before continuing. '*One*: yesterday was hardly World War 3. You had a fight – so what? You've been best friends for years!'

'But she's really mad at me,' Ivy whispered.

'And *two*,' Brendan continued, 'it doesn't matter how mad either of you might be right now. You are too good a friend to let Sophia humiliate herself again!'

Ivy breathed in deeply. *He's right*, she realised. Maybe Sophia would be mad that she'd come. Maybe they'd even have another fight. But they had been friends for too long to let one fight change everything.

'OK,' said Ivy, grabbing her boot from under the bed. She found its twin by the chest of drawers, already pointing at the door. 'I'll be there as fast as I can,' she promised.

. . . Or, as fast as the bus will take me!

🦇 🦇 🦇

Half an hour later, she was crossing the park at top speed, aiming for Gingham Central – the skatepark. She came to a dead halt when she caught sight of Sophia.

What does she think she's doing?

Looking more confident on her skateboard than Ivy had ever seen her before, Sophia zoomed straight off the edge of one of the skatepark's concrete canyons. She looped through mid-air in a fast somersault that made Ivy's heart lurch. A moment later, she landed – almost perfectly.

Wow. Ivy drew a deep breath, feeling relief shudder through her. *OK, maybe Sophia won't end up in the ER after all.*

She started forwards . . . but Sophia hadn't finished. She flashed a quick look at Finn from underneath her newly blonde fringe, then launched herself forwards again, flinging herself into the air off the top of the canyon. This time, her loop soared even higher. She gripped the sides of her skateboard to carry it with her as she flew . . .

But skateboards hadn't been designed for vampire strength.

Beneath Sophia's grip, the skateboard snapped with a crack that echoed through the park.

With a shriek, Ivy started running. But even her vampire speed would not have got her there in time.

As the two pieces fell apart, Sophia tumbled through the air and landed hard on her back in the grass nearby.

Ivy and Brendan were the first to reach her, as people ran from all over the park.

'Sophia!' Ivy bent over her friend, shaking with panic.

'I'm OK,' Sophia mumbled, her eyes flickering

open. She gave Ivy a weak smile as she pulled herself up to a sitting position. 'Seriously.'

'Thank darkness.' Ivy let out her breath. Then she lowered her voice to a hiss. '*What were you thinking?*'

Before Sophia could answer, though, Finn came running.

'Are you OK? I've never seen a skateboard snap like that!' He picked up the broken pieces, shaking his head while his followers gathered around him to stare at the evidence. 'Talk about amateur workmanship!'

'Oh . . . right!' Sophia's eyes widened as she gazed up at Finn. 'And I'm fine. Absolutely fine!'

Over Sophia's shoulder, Brendan met Ivy's gaze. She sighed and gave him a discreet nod. *We lucked out*, she admitted to herself. All the skaters gathering round were blaming the skateboard. It hadn't even occurred to them that Sophia might have been super-strong.

But didn't Sophia even realise what a close call it had been? What she'd done hadn't just put herself at risk – it had put *every* vampire at risk! She'd nearly exploded vampire secrets wide open . . . but she was so busy looking starry-eyed at Finn, she didn't even seem to have noticed.

Gritting her teeth, Ivy grabbed Sophia's arm. 'Come on,' she growled. 'We need to get you home.'

'No way. I'm fine!' Sophia tried to yank her arm away, but she couldn't help wincing.

'You're definitely bruised, and you need a rest.' Brendan took Sophia's other arm.

Pouting, Sophia stopped resisting. As Ivy and Brendan drew her away from the broken pieces of the skateboard, she whispered, 'What are you *doing?* Couldn't you see? Finn was *talking to me*! Isn't that fantastic?'

'*Fantastic?*' Ivy had to drop Sophia's arm before she could give in and shake her own best

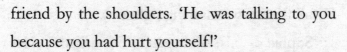

friend by the shoulders. 'He was talking to you because you had hurt yourself!'

Sophia gave a wistful sigh. 'He was worried about me. Wasn't that sweet of him?'

'Not sweet enough to justify *actual* bruises,' said Ivy. 'You seriously –'

She stopped abruptly as her vampire hearing picked up on the conversation going on among the skater-boys behind them.

'How crazy is that Franklin Grove girl?' said one of the boys. 'Watch out, Finn. Who knows what she'll try next to get your attention?'

'She obviously likes you a *scary* lot, bro,' said another boy. 'If she's putting this much effort into faking –'

The first boy snorted. 'Did you see that "accidental" triple somersault earlier?'

Ivy winced as she tried to imagine how much a triple somersault would hurt even a vampire.

Probably not nearly as much as hearing what

Finn's friends were saying right now.

'Sophia . . .' she began, in a whisper. Her friend's face was pale and she looked as though she felt sick.

But Finn suddenly broke in: 'Lay off her, you guys! You don't have to be jerks about it.'

Score one for Skater Finn, Ivy thought.

Maybe he wasn't the right boy for her best friend . . . but he wasn't a bad guy, after all.

'Hey!' Finn called from behind them. Ivy turned and saw that he had broken away from his friends to head straight for Sophia. He held out his skateboard, which was painted with swirls of yellow and bright orange. 'Here. This is one of my favourites. Do you want to borrow it until you get a new one?'

'Really?' Sophia breathed. She took the board from him and stroked it reverentially. 'You would really do that? For me?'

'Hey, it's no big deal.' Finn shrugged. 'I've got more of them at home.'

He's telling the truth, Ivy realised, as she looked at his expression.

To Finn, it really was no big deal. He was just a nice guy, doing a nice thing. But to Sophia . . . Ivy's chest tightened.

Sophia was so busy stroking the skateboard, she hadn't even noticed how casual Finn was being. And to her, the gesture obviously meant a *lot*.

As Finn headed back towards his friends, Ivy tried to think of the right thing to say. She had to tell Sophia the truth somehow, but she couldn't bear to break her best friend's heart by doing it. How would Olivia put it?

It had to be gentle, it had to be kind . . .

'Did you see how stupid she looked?'

The biting tones of one of the identical pixie-cut blonde skater-girls on the other side of the park sliced right into Ivy's vampire-strong hearing. 'She doesn't just go head-over-heels on her skateboard – she's going head-over-heels for Finn, too!'

The other skater-girls giggled.

'She's like a little panting puppy,' one of them agreed. '"*Oh, Finn, just look at me, please look at me, please!*"'

'He must feel *so* sorry for her!' a third girl piped in.

Sophia let out a muffled gasp of hurt, and Ivy could already feel the death-squint on her face as she spun around.

No one makes fun of my best friend. Especially not some identikit blonde clone!

She started forwards, like a warrior going into battle, but Sophia's hand clamped around her arm.

'No!' Sophia's face looked almost green against her pixie-cut blonde hair now, but she shook her head. '*Think* about it, Ivy. A human wouldn't have heard what they were saying. They're too far away.'

'She's right,' Brendan agreed. His jaw was clenched with obvious frustration, but he shook his head at Ivy.

'I don't care!' Ivy glared at the skater-girls across the field. 'I'm going to go over there and tell those little clones exactly what I think of them.'

'This is Lincoln Vale,' Sophia said. 'You can't just march over there and call out the mean girls. *These* mean girls aren't used to being overheard from far away, like girls in Franklin Grove are. They'll know that something's not right.' She took a deep breath. 'Remember what we were told before we started this school? We need to be careful.'

Ivy closed her eyes and felt frustration sweep through her. But Sophia was right.

Slowly, with dragging steps, she turned back

to her friends and started walking away from the skatepark.

High school sucks, she thought. *And not in a good way!*

Brendan took her hand and squeezed it, while Sophia walked stiff-backed beside her, cradling Finn's skateboard under one arm.

As they reached the gates of the park, they saw a familiar, black-clad figure passing between them. Ivy nearly groaned. Of all the times to run into Goth-Queen Amelia!

Amelia barely spared them a glance before narrowing her eyes at the skater-girls across the park. 'I saw those idiotic girls laughing at you,' she snapped. 'Do *not* let that continue. Otherwise it'll follow all of us into school! If you want to be goths, you need to assert yourselves.'

Only Brendan's meaningful hand-squeeze stopped Ivy from snapping right back, *I'll show you assertiveness!*

Amelia strode past without waiting for a reply. Ivy turned to glare after her, and saw the older girl head for her usual lounging spot, just by the skate-area. Her followers were already flocking there from the four corners of the park.

Actually, wait a minute . . . Ivy frowned as the thought finally occurred to her. *If Amelia's so determined to preserve goth social dominance, then why does she spend so much time at the skatepark?* Amelia seemed to come here almost as much as Sophia! She thought back to the time that Amelia had been in the park, watching Sophia with undisguised suspicion. Watching Sophia and *Finn* . . .

Ivy narrowed her eyes in suspicion as she watched Amelia sit down on the grass less than fifteen feet from the concrete canyons. *Something fishy is definitely going on*, Ivy thought. *Something fishy that's wearing black!*

Chapter Nine

'Pardon?' Olivia bit back a yawn just in time. As her interviewer beamed at her, she tried to clear her head, which was foggy with exhaustion. Plus, she was feeling faint again from the corset she was wearing beneath her lavender silk ballgown for this on-set interview. 'Could you repeat the question, please?'

'Of course.' The interviewer, a sleek, dark-haired British woman in a form-fitting pencil skirt and blouse, smiled at her condescendingly. 'This is your first interview for a DVD special feature, isn't it? You must be so nervous, you poor thing.'

'A little bit,' Olivia said, smiling politely for

the sake of the rolling cameras. Inside her head, though, she answered more honestly: *I'm more fed up than nervous!* She had barely slept the last two nights. Now it was Monday, her final day in England, and she was wasting her last precious hours with this interview. Jackson was packing his suitcases somewhere nearby, preparing for his return flight to Hollywood *that night*!

How was she supposed to concentrate on a silly DVD interview when she might be losing her last chance to make things right between them?

'And will you be doing it again?' the interviewer asked. She cocked one eyebrow. 'What exactly do you see as your future in Hollywood?'

Uh-oh. Olivia swallowed, trying to maintain a pleasant expression. Ever since she'd arrived on-set, she'd been asking herself the same question, but she still hadn't come up with an answer. Could she do it now, while the cameras were rolling?

'Well,' she said slowly, 'acting *is* something that

I truly love doing . . . but it is a lot of work, and there's a lot of stress involved in working on a film set.'

The interviewer smiled. 'You're certainly not leading an ordinary teenager's life.'

That's exactly the problem, Olivia thought. She just *knew* that if she and Jackson were two normal teenagers, nothing could stand in their way. But they weren't 'normal' and that meant –

No! With sudden resolution, she cut off the familiar chain of worries before it could even begin. *I can't just keep asking myself the same questions again and again. I have to do something! If I don't, I'll regret it forever.*

Olivia tried to draw a deep breath to brace herself – then winced, as the tight corset bit into her side. She managed to force a smile as she answered the interviewer's question:

'No, it's not an ordinary life,' she said. 'But it's the one I've chosen . . . for now.'

I'm going to find Jackson and have an honest, face-to-face conversation. I will get my future cleared up once and for all . . . even if I have to wear a hoop-skirt as I do it!

🦇 　　 🦇 　　 🦇

The interview seemed to go on forever, but finally she was free. Olivia hurried to Jackson's trailer. She paused outside, took a deep breath, and knocked. She was already practising her opening line.

Then her shoulders sagged as the silence stretched on. *What good is an opening line if he doesn't even answer the door?*

Biting her lip, Olivia thought it through. Jackson often wore headphones when he was alone. He probably just hadn't heard her. She couldn't give up now!

Tentatively, she turned the handle of the trailer door. It opened a crack . . . and she let out her held breath.

The trailer was empty.

Of course. Jackson must be in the Hair and Make-up trailer, getting ready to shoot his last scene!

She was just turning to leave when she caught sight of something flickering inside the trailer. It was his laptop computer, flashing a warning – it needed to be plugged in to charge.

Olivia hesitated. She didn't want to invade his privacy . . . but she knew how hard he'd been working on . . . *something* . . . lately. She didn't want him to lose whatever it was, if the computer shut itself off.

I just won't look at anything, she promised herself. She eased herself into the trailer, careful not to knock anything over with the massive hoop-skirt of her Victorian ballgown.

At the last moment, though, as she was leaning over to plug in the laptop, she couldn't help herself – she caught a glimpse of the email Jackson had been in the middle of writing.

She jerked her eyes away quickly . . . but there

had only been one line written so far, and it had already burned itself into her brain.

I just don't know what to do about

. . . *Me?* Olivia silently wondered.

Her heartbeat was thundering in her ears as she backed hastily away from the computer.

Had Jackson been writing to someone about her? Was the reason he hadn't said anything decisive . . . because he was *nervous*?

Olivia shook her head. She'd always seen Jackson as being so confident . . . but inside, what if he was just as unsure about her feelings as she was about his?

All this time, she'd been waiting for him to make a gesture . . . but now it felt like the time for Olivia to make a gesture for *him*.

🦇 🦇 🦇

By the time she reached the Hair and Make-up trailer, Olivia was light-headed with panic and possibility. *Can I really do this?*

She looked through the door and saw Jackson sitting with his back to her, familiar and perfect. No one else was there to overhear them. It was the perfect moment.

Olivia set one hand on her stomach, trying to settle the nerves fluttering there. *I can do this . . . for him.*

'Hey,' she said, speaking quickly. 'Whatever I'm about to say, just *please* don't try to stop me. I have to get this out, or I'll burst!'

Even as she saw his shoulders stiffen with shock, her words tumbled out. 'I love you. I *do*! And I'm sorry things are so difficult. I have to be totally honest and say I just don't know if I'm going to be doing many more movies in the near future.'

She had to stop for a quick breath, almost panting in the tight corset. *What on earth did Victorian ladies do when they got emotional?* Ignoring the tightness in her waist, she carried on: 'I'm pretty sure fourteen-year-olds aren't meant to be *this* tired! I mean, I think you're amazing for being able to do it, but . . . it's just not for me. And I don't want to be part of an "it" couple. I want to be a normal boy's normal girlfriend!'

She sighed. 'Obviously, I know *that's* not going to happen. You're way too famous! But . . .' She paused, closing her eyes as she finished: 'I really think we should give us another try . . . Do you?'

There was a long, terrifying silence. Finally, Olivia opened her eyes.

Jackson had turned around . . . Except, it wasn't Jackson. It was Will.

'Oh, stake me now!' Olivia gasped.

Will frowned. 'Huh?'

'Nothing,' Olivia replied, realising that she could not very well explain to him that she had blurted out something that her vampire twin sister did when she was mortified. Spots danced in front of her eyes. Was it possible to faint from sheer embarrassment? She looked down at the ridiculous *prison* of fabric that she was wearing and wondered, didn't she see historical women in movies reach for paper fans at times of distress? Where was *Olivia's* paper fan?

Then she burst out laughing, and put her face in her hands. *This is the kind of thing that could* only *happen to me*, she thought, shaking her head.

'I'm sorry,' said Will, his face flushed as he stood up from his chair. 'I just didn't know how to interrupt you once you'd got started.' Then he smiled ruefully. 'So . . . I guess you're the ultimate fangirl, huh?'

Olivia's jaw dropped open. She stared at him in pure horror. 'Is that . . .?' She croaked the words. 'Is that what Jackson told you?'

'No! That was just a dumb joke. Sorry.' Will ran a hand through his hair, in a scarily Jackson-like gesture. 'Listen, that guy does *not* shut up about you – like, *ever.*'

Olivia blinked, trying to take that in. 'Really?'

'Really,' Will said. 'And hey, look on the bright side . . . at least you got to have a dress rehearsal. Can I give you some advice?'

Olivia nodded dumbly.

Will smiled. 'Repeat that whole speech to Jackson. Don't change a word. Now, go get him!'

Olivia staggered out of the make-up trailer, desperately trying to run through exactly what she'd said in the 'dress rehearsal'. But she could barely remember any of it now!

I can't do it again. Not yet! She aimed for her own trailer, trying to stay upright. *I'll just take a minute, have a drink of water . . . get myself together. Then I'll go find Jackson.*

She swallowed hard. It looked like she'd be improvising again. But at least, next time, she'd be aiming her declaration of love at the right boy!

Please let it work.

She opened the door to her trailer and was overwhelmed by the smell of . . .

Roses . . . Lots and *lots* of roses! As Olivia stepped inside, she gazed around in shock.

Her whole trailer had been transformed into a rippling river of beautiful red and white rose petals. *Romantic* rose petals, everywhere!

They covered her table, her chairs and the carpet, while twelve long-stemmed red roses lay on the side-table by the trailer door.

In one corner sat her laptop, with red-and-white rose petals scattered across its keyboard. As she stepped into the trailer, the laptop screen came to life, playing a pre-recorded message, but she barely even noticed. Ivy and Brendan were yelling, 'Congratulations on wrapping your first ever shoot! We can't wait to see you!' from the screen – but Olivia couldn't even see them through the mist of tears that had formed in her eyes.

She couldn't even take in the words that Camilla and her bio-dad added to the message as they appeared on-screen.

All of Olivia's attention was on the river of rose petals . . . and the sudden feeling that someone else had just entered the trailer.

Slowly, she turned round, hardly daring to hope. But there he stood, with a suitcase at his feet – the boy she'd been looking for all day.

Jackson gave her a slow smile.

Chapter Ten

Ivy almost laughed when she walked past the crowd of blonde skater-girls outside school on Monday morning. They had all turned at exactly the same moment to glare at her, just as if they shared some kind of hive-mind underneath their identical pixie-cuts.

Don't worry, clones, she thought, rolling her eyes. *I have absolutely zero interest in poaching your skater king.*

All that Ivy cared about was Sophia . . . who hadn't been on the school bus. *Again.* Worse, Ivy hadn't seen Sophia skating along the sidewalk, either.

Please don't let her have had another crazy accident! she prayed. Surely, after yesterday, her best friend would have finally had the sense to give up being a wannabe skater-girl?

Up ahead, she saw Brendan standing near the school doorway, talking to Amelia Thompson. Ivy sighed but forced a polite smile for the Goth-Queen.

'Ivy.' Amelia nodded back with her usual cool courtesy. 'I see you were getting a few dirty looks back there. Don't let those skater-girls get to you. Or at least . . .' She frowned slightly. 'Don't *show* it if they do.'

'Got it,' Ivy said, and bit back a reluctant smile.

Goth or bunny, it seemed that all popular girls had at least one thing in common . . . an *obsession* with image!

As Amelia headed inside, Ivy whispered to Brendan, 'Have you seen Sophia?'

Brendan shook his head. Holding out his hand

to her, he asked, 'What about you? Are you ready for another week of being part of the "it crowd"?'

'Oh, gak.' Ivy pretended to gag. 'Let me think. New school, new students, and a rulebook I don't seem to have . . .'

'Look at it this way.' Brendan grinned at her, giving her hand a warm squeeze. 'If you don't follow the "rules", then that must mean you're a *true* outsider here.'

Slowly, a grin spread over Ivy's face. 'Huh . . . You're right, I am. Just the way I like it!'

She leaned forwards to give Brendan a hug . . . but he stopped her by nodding over her shoulder. 'Here comes Sophia.'

Ivy's heart sank. From the expression on Brendan's face, the outlook wasn't good. She turned, bracing herself to see a picture of Finn's skateboard tattooed on to Sophia's face, or something equally ridiculous.

But, a second later, Ivy was letting out a

sigh of relief. Her best friend was wearing a fashionable, halter-neck black dress. Her black, bat earrings might look unexpected against her pixie-cut blonde hair, but otherwise she looked back to normal.

She didn't look happy, though.

'Are you OK?' Ivy hurried over to her, looking for new bruises. 'Did you have another accident? Or –'

'No.' Sophia sighed and gave a lopsided smile. 'Although I did think for a minute that my eardrums might have exploded when my parents saw my new hairstyle.'

'Ouch.' Ivy winced, putting a supportive hand on her friend's arm. 'They didn't like it?'

Sophia shook her head. 'I'm pretty sure I'm grounded until *Christmas*.'

Ivy stared at her. 'You're kidding. They actually *grounded* you?'

'They said I should have asked permission

first. You were right. I guess I just . . .' Sophia's voice drifted off as she glanced over at where Finn stood with his 'bodacious' buddies just inside the hallway. She sighed.

One of them looked back at her and laughed.

Ivy's teeth clenched together. 'That's it. I'm going to take care of this once and for all!'

Before either of her friends could stop her, she marched down the hall. Bunnies scattered out of her way, clearing a path, and she had to admit . . . it felt good.

Not that she would ever scatter bunnies on purpose.

'Hey!' she snarled, as she reached Finn and his crew. 'I need to talk to you.'

Standing in the middle of the skater crowd, Finn looked nervous. 'Is something wrong?'

'In *private*,' Ivy said, and gave Finn's snickering friends a death-squint. They turned pale, and edged away.

Sneering at them, Ivy pulled Finn away with her. 'Look,' she said in a fierce undertone. 'I know you're not the brightest crayon in the box –'

'Sorry?' His face creased into a frown. 'Have we actually *met*?'

Ivy rolled her eyes. 'The point is, though, I didn't think you were a total *jerk*.'

'What?' He flinched as if he'd been slapped. 'I'm not. Why would you think I am?'

Ivy pointed at the skater group waiting for him. 'Can't you see how cruel your friends are being to Sophia? Why don't you stop them?'

His frown deepened. 'Well . . .'

Ivy lowered her voice to a whisper. 'And, anyway, what are you *doing*, giving Sophia skateboards to borrow? Can't you see she's crushing on you? Are you actually *trying* to lead her on, or do you just not care about her feelings?'

'I'm not trying to lead her on,' he said. His frown had eased, but he was flushed now with what looked like embarrassment. 'I wouldn't do that. It's not my style.'

'Hmm,' Ivy said sceptically.

'And as for my friends . . .' Finn sighed, tapping his skateboard against his side. 'I'm sorry they've been uncool. I'll talk to them, though. I *will*.' He squared his shoulders. 'I'll make it clear that they need to leave Sophia alone. She's a nice girl, and she doesn't deserve to be unhappy.'

Finn's voice softened as he seemed to catch sight of someone over Ivy's shoulder. His eyes turned dreamy. 'Believe me,' he finished in a whisper. 'I *know* how she feels. Crushing on someone who doesn't feel the same . . . it's rough.'

Ivy twisted around to follow his gaze – and had to snap her mouth shut to hold back a gasp.

Amelia was sauntering into Homeroom, tall and arrogant in full goth-splendour . . . and Finn was gazing after her wistfully!

Ivy suddenly felt dizzy. *The skater boy has a thing for the Goth Queen? High school is even weirder than I'd thought!*

She forced herself to think through what Finn had just told her. 'OK,' she said. 'I accept that you're not actually trying to hurt Sophia. But . . .' She narrowed her eyes in a medium-level death-squint. 'Promise me you'll be more sensitive in the future.'

'Absolutely,' Finn said. He raised one hand to high-five her.

Grimacing, Ivy accepted the high-five. As he went back to the crowd of skater guys and *SkaterGirl 2.0* clones, she walked slowly back to her own group. Sophia was watching her carefully.

'What did he say?' she asked, the moment Ivy caught up with her.

Ivy shook her head. 'It doesn't matter. All you need to know is that Finn is going to be nice to you from now on, and his friends won't tease you any more.'

'Finn's always been nice to me!' Sophia protested. Ivy could hear the desperation in her friend's voice.

Gently, she put her arm around Sophia's shoulders. 'Yes, but he's not . . . *right* for you.' These were hard words to say out loud and Ivy didn't like hurting Sophia's feelings, but she knew it was time for this madness to end. Things could have been worse. At least Finn wasn't a complete jerk. It turned out Sophia had good taste – even if it was misplaced.

'Don't forget the Second Law,' Ivy mumbled to Sophia, out of anyone else's hearing. '"No vampire should fall in –"'

'I know,' Sophia interrupted her, nodding sadly. 'Being with Finn was just a silly fantasy.'

Ivy felt a twist of pain at the wrecked look on her friend's face. *First crushes are never easy!*

'I'm sorry,' she said. 'And I'm really sorry if I've been annoying you this last week. I was only trying to help.'

'I know.' Sophia's eyes brimmed with tears. 'Starting a new school is just so confusing. I'm going to need my sidekick.'

'No doubt,' said Ivy, feeling the sting of tears in her own eyes. 'But, wait . . . when did *I* become the sidekick?'

Sophia laughed, and pulled Ivy into a hug. Just then, someone walked up to them. It was a tall goth-boy Ivy hadn't seen before, dressed in a black Pall Bearers T-shirt and ripped black jeans. But it wasn't his clothing that caught Ivy's eye, it was his hair – his *bleached blond* hair.

He stopped beside them, looked Sophia up and down . . . and gave her a nod of deep respect.

Sophia's mouth dropped open as he walked away.

'See?' Ivy whispered. Grinning, she poked Sophia's arm. 'I'm not the only one who thinks so!'

But there was no time for Sophia to reply. Suddenly, they were being swarmed by goths.

'Oh, my Goooood!' A pale, black-haired goth-girl clutched at her heart. 'Baxter actually acknowledged you!'

'He nodded *right at you*,' agreed a skinny goth-boy beside her. He gazed at Sophia in worshipful awe. 'Do you have any idea *how cool* you must be?'

Grinning, Ivy stepped back, letting Sophia be the centre of attention. Goths on all sides were inviting her to parties, asking her advice . . . and completely ignoring Ivy. This was just the way she liked it. She watched as Sophia answered question after question, clearly thriving under all the attention. At one moment, she caught Ivy's eye and the two of them shared a secret glance of pleasure. It was so nice for Ivy to see her friend looking happy again.

'Excuse me,' a student said, squeezing past Ivy to get closer to Sophia. 'I just want to get to the popular girl.'

Ivy made a show of stepping aside. 'Be my guest,' she said, with a proud smile.

'Hey.' Brendan stepped up behind her to murmur into her ear. 'Just so you know? As far as I'm concerned, *you* are still the coolest girl in the world. Even if your hairstyle is no longer the "in"-thing . . .'

'Oh, shut up.' Laughing, Ivy turned and threw her arms around him.

Over his shoulder, she took another look around the darkened halls of Franklin Grove High. Students milled around in their groups, chatting happily.

High school was definitely weird . . . but maybe it *wouldn't* eat her alive, after all. If anything, she was now intrigued. Over in one corner of the hallway stood Finn with his friends. He was staring hard at another place in the hall, where Amelia's goth pals crowded around her.

A star-crossed romance, Ivy thought. *Even I'm curious to see how this will end . . .*

Olivia looked up into Jackson's face, which was more gorgeous than the sea of red petals in her trailer. She felt as if she were in a waking dream. 'You did this . . . for me?'

He nodded. For once, he wasn't wearing his megastar smile. He looked nervous . . . and vulnerable. He pulled away from her. 'Of course,' he said, and swallowed visibly. 'I thought you knew how I felt about you?'

'I didn't,' Olivia said softly.

But now . . .

Suddenly, so many things made sense. She understood why he'd wanted to walk by the river together, and why he'd organised the private lunch on the London eye. She knew now why

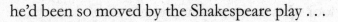

he'd been so moved by the Shakespeare play . . .

She knew everything!

They were gazing into each other's eyes, so intensely that Olivia could hardly breathe. Now was the perfect time for her 'spontaneous' speech . . . but, right now, she couldn't find the words!

Oh no! She grabbed a rose from the side-table by the door and pretended to inhale deeply, to hide her face.

Unfortunately, she breathed a bit *too* deeply. The strong scent made her choke! She doubled over, coughing. As her eyes watered, Jackson hurried over to slap her back.

Argh! Waving him off, she straightened up. 'Why,' she gasped, 'can I never do these scenes properly in real life?'

'Don't ask me.' Jackson was smiling again. 'I can't see a single thing wrong with the way you're playing this one. You know, you've never looked as pretty as you do right now.'

Olivia snorted. 'What, because of my red, watering eyes and flushed face?'

Jackson reached out and stroked a strand of hair away from her face. 'No,' he whispered. 'Because I had to spend *so* much time away from you to realise how beautiful you are . . . inside and out.'

Olivia *couldn't* keep it inside any longer. She had to tell him. Right now . . .

But Jackson got there first. 'I love you.'

As relief and joy rippled through her, Olivia felt all the tension she'd been carrying around for weeks simply disappear. It was the easiest thing she had ever done to reply: 'I love you too.'

Jackson's lips curved into a smile that had nothing to do with Hollywood . . . and everything to do with her. As his warm arms wrapped around her again, Olivia knew down to her bones that, somehow, everything was going to work out just fine.

I can't wait to tell Ivy!

🦇

Six hours later, Ivy was grinning as she sat at her computer, talking to her twin on Lonely Echo. 'You're kidding,' she said. 'You actually confessed your love to his *body double*? How alike *are* they? I mean, if Jackson's busy, does Will go to his doctor's appointments for him?'

'Oh, hush!' said Olivia, but she was laughing. She looked cosy in a fluffy pink bathrobe, her legs tucked up beneath her on what looked like a very plush hotel bed. 'You're just lucky I can laugh about it now. For the first couple of hours after it happened, I almost fainted every time I thought of it.'

Ivy laughed as she scooped up another spoonful of her after-school Marshmallow Platelets. 'So, I guess, all's well that ends well, right?'

'Totally.' Olivia beamed out from the computer screen. 'Everything's absolutely perfect with Jackson . . . and I'm not leaving Franklin Grove.'

'Really and truly?' Ivy set down her cereal. 'You're not going to get talked into moving to Hollywood and enjoying the high life once *Eternal Sunset* is done?'

'Nope.' Olivia shook her head firmly. 'The moment this shoot wraps, I'm coming back to Franklin Grove – for good.'

'That is the best news *ever*.' Contentment flooded through Ivy as she took it in.

With Olivia around, even Franklin Grove High might start to feel even more normal. And life was always better with her twin. Then a thought occurred to her.

'But what about your rekindled romance?' she asked. 'Isn't that going to be difficult with you in Franklin Grove and Jackson going to film sets all over the world?'

Olivia shrugged. She didn't look unhappy. 'We've learnt a lot from last time,' she said. 'We're going to make much more of an effort to make time for each other.'

Ivy settled back on her chair. 'Tell me the story again,' she said. 'Exactly as it happened.'

Olivia looked surprised. 'Ivy Vega, are you becoming a die-hard romantic?'

Ivy felt herself wriggle with embarrassment. 'Never! Don't ever say that in front of anyone else. I just . . . you know . . . want to make sure you don't forget any crucial detail. You'll probably be telling this story to your grandchildren, so you want to get it right!'

The two of them burst out laughing, then Olivia cleared her throat, ready to repeat the story. It was a good one, after all . . .

FASHION FRIGHTMARE!

Readers, I have such an exciting piece for you in this month's issue of VAMP magazine! Our very own star journo with the bluest vampire blood running through her veins – yes, Ivy Vega – has agreed to write a piece on vampire fashion for all those young and hip readers out there. I know you're reading, don't try to pretend you're not!

Apparently, there's this trend called 'refashioning', and Ivy likes to refashion T-shirts for going to Pall Bearer concerts. Shudder. Personally, I can't stand their yowling, but these bands are all the rage. As are Ivy's outfits! Readers, brace yourself for some fashion magic – over to you, Ivy.

Signing off,

Georgia Huntingdon, Editor in Chief

When Georgia invited me to write about fashion for VAMP, I felt like someone had put a stake through my heart. Me, Ivy Vega? Fashion? Give me a break. Yeah, my twin thinks the mall is heavenly. Olivia will buy anything that is pink or has a rhinestone glued to it. Not me. I like to make my own statement. Which got me thinking...

Whenever the Pall Bearers are in town, I get the gang together and we all have a total Fright Night customising our own T-shirts to wear to the concert. I know that there have to be other teen vampires out there who like to put their own goth spin on what they wear.

So if you think you can totally rock red – blood red! – get your gear together and get ready to make this cool coffin-logo T-shirt . . .

Materials Needed

- White or cream T-shirt, freshly laundered and pressed

- Suitable work surface

- Newspaper

- Paint brush

- 25mm-wide masking tape

- Measuring tape

- Red fabric paint

- Tailor's chalk, or washable coloured pencil or pen

Ivy's Instructions

First you need to get prepared.

🦇   Lay your T-shirt flat on a newspaper-covered work surface.

🦇   Put another piece of old newspaper between the front and back of the T-shirt. (This is to protect the back of your T-shirt from any fabric paint leaking through.) Smooth out any wrinkles in the fabric.

This 'refashioning' project features a funky coffin painted in red, so first you've got to mark out the coffin shape using masking tape. Then you get to paint it in!

🦇 First, find the centre of your T-shirt by measuring across the front from the base of one armhole to the other. Divide this measurement in two. For example, if the measurement across is 30 cm, your centre point will be at 15 cm.

🦇 Draw a little 'X' here using your tailor's chalk or washable coloured pencil, about 5 cm down from the neckline, to mark the centre.

🦇 Cut a 7 cm piece of masking tape and stick it down horizontally, centred below the X. This first piece of masking tape will mark the top of your coffin shape.

Now it's time mark out the first two sides and base of the coffin.

🦇 Measure 10 cm down the middle of the

T-shirt, starting from the top edge of your piece of masking tape. Mark place with an X. Measure 10 cm out to the left of this X and mark place with another X.

Measure 10 cm out to the right of your centre X and draw another X. You should now have three Xs in a straight line across the middle of your T-shirt.

Cut two pieces of masking tape 13.5 cm long and place each on the diagonal from the corners of the top piece of masking tape to the Xs on either far side. Now you've got your top two sides marked out.

To find the bottom of your coffin shape, measure 23 cm down from the centre X and draw one last X. Cut a 5 cm long piece of tape and stick it down horizontally, centred below this bottom X.

Now for the final two sides of your coffin.

🦇   Cut two 25 cm pieces of masking tape and lay them diagonally from each outer point to each side of the bottom piece of masking tape.

Woohoo! You have made a coffin shape! That's the tricky part done. You should have something like this:

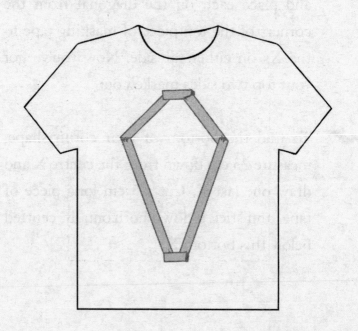

Now mark a 1 cm border all the way around the outer edge of your coffin shape, using your tailor's chalk or pencil.

Apply a second set of masking tape around the outside of the border you've marked. You don't need to measure the tape lengths as carefully this time, just ensure that all lengths of tape overlap. Like this:

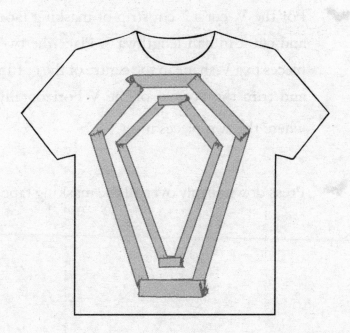

Now it's time to add a 'V for Vega' shape to the centre of your coffin!

(Though, if you prefer, you can make your own initial out of masking tape. Apologies to anyone whose name begins with Q . . . You could be in for a long afternoon.)

- For the V, cut a 7 cm strip of masking tape and cut it in half lengthways. Place the two pieces in a V-shape in the centre of the coffin and trim the bottom of the V horizontally where the two pieces meet.

- Press down firmly over all the masking tape.

Your T-shirt should now look a little something like this:

OK, now it's painting time!

🦇 Shake your bottle of fabric paint and remove the lid.

🦇 With a paint brush, apply an even layer of red paint to all fabric inside the masking tape.

(A note to all you vamps out there: you'll probably get very hungry right about now. Red paint looks a lot like blood, so it's a good idea to scarf some Marshmallow Platelets before beginning!)

Still have some red paint left? You could splatter a few blood drops on your T-shirt:

🦇 CAUTION! Make sure there is nothing nearby that might get ruined by a few drops of red fabric paint. Clear the vampire decks!

- Dip your paintbrush into the paint. Don't overload your brush. Hold the brush near a corner of your T-shirt. Pull on the brush bristles and release. Spatters of 'blood' should go across your fabric.

- Repeat as necessary. Now go and wash your hands!

- Replace the lid on your jar of fabric paint, wash your paintbrush(es) and leave your T-shirt to dry. It should need about three hours, but I like to leave it overnight.

- Once your T-shirt is completely dry, remove all masking tape. Get an adult to press your T-shirt with a hot iron to seal the colour and it's done!

You're all ready to go to a Pall Bearers concert and scream with all your might!

Check back next time for more top do-it-yourself tips, fashion fans!

Discover the fangtastic new series from Sienna Mercer...These twins will have you howling with laughter!

To their classmates, Daniel and Justin are identical twin brothers. But in fact they couldn't be more different.

On their thirteenth birthday, one of them is destined to turn into a werewolf... This full moon is going to change everything!

EGMONT PRESS: ETHICAL PUBLISHING

Egmont Press is about turning writers into successful authors and children into passionate readers – producing books that enrich and entertain. As a responsible children's publisher, we go even further, considering the world in which our consumers are growing up.

Safety First
Naturally, all of our books meet legal safety requirements. But we go further than this; every book with play value is tested to the highest standards – if it fails, it's back to the drawing-board.

Made Fairly
We are working to ensure that the workers involved in our supply chain – the people that make our books – are treated with fairness and respect.

Responsible Forestry
We are committed to ensuring all our papers come from environmentally and socially responsible forest sources.

For more information, please visit our website at
www.egmont.co.uk/ethical